"Everyone has secrets... they share with those... prefer to keep to themselves."

Wyatt was quiet for a long moment. "I hope you know that if you ever want to share yours, you can trust me."

Rosa trusted very few people. And she certainly wasn't going to trust Wyatt, who was only a temporary tenant and would be out of her life in a few short weeks.

"If I had any secrets, I might do that. But I don't. I'm a completely open book."

She tried for a breezy smile but could tell he wasn't at all convinced. In fact, he looked slightly disappointed.

She tried to ignore her guilt and opted to change the subject instead. "The lightning seems to have stopped for now. I am sure the power will be back on soon."

"No doubt."

"Thank you again for coming to my rescue. Good night. Be careful going back down the stairs."

"I will do that. Good night."

He studied her, his features unreadable in the dim light of her flashlight. As he turned to go back down the stairs, the masculine scent of him swirled to her. She felt again that sudden wild urge to kiss him but ignored it. Instead, she went into her darkened apartment, her dog at her heels, and firmly closed the door behind her. If only she could close the door to her thoughts as easily.

THE WOMEN OF BRAMBLEBERRY HOUSE

Dear Reader,

Several years ago (2007, to be exact!) I wrote a book called *Shelter from the Storm*. This was a romantic suspense about a small-town doctor and the local sheriff in Utah who work together to rescue a terrified fifteen-year-old girl from a dark and terrible situation. In the process, the doctor and the sheriff fall in love (of course!) and end up providing a warm, supportive home for the girl. I loved writing this book and still get reader emails about it. Many readers who have read *Shelter from the Storm* have begged me to write a story for the rescued girl, Rosa Galvez. I'm so happy I finally had the chance with *A Brambleberry Summer*!

Rosa Galvez is a heroine who has faced unimaginable pain and loss. She has managed to build a happy life for herself on the Oregon Coast while keeping her past to herself, until a single father and his adorable son who have suffered their own loss move into Brambleberry House.

I loved returning to this beautiful part of the world and the charms of this historic house at the seaside, and it was such a delight to finally give Rosa the joy and happiness she so deserves.

Happy reading!

RaeAnne

RaeAnne Thayne

A BRAMBLEBERRY SUMMER

HARLEQUIN
SPECIAL
EDITION

HARLEQUIN®
SPECIAL
EDITION™

Recycling programs
for this product may
not exist in your area.

ISBN-13: 978-1-335-40791-7

A Brambleberry Summer

Copyright © 2021 by RaeAnne Thayne LLC

Harlequin Enterprises ULC
22 Adelaide St. West, 40th Floor
Toronto, Ontario M5H 4E3, Canada
www.Harlequin.com

Printed in U.S.A.

New York Times bestselling author **RaeAnne Thayne** finds inspiration in the beautiful northern Utah mountains, where she lives with her family. Her books have won numerous honors, including six RITA® Award nominations from Romance Writers of America and Career Achievement and Romance Pioneer Awards from *RT Book Reviews*. She loves to hear from readers and can be reached through her website at raeannethayne.com.

To all the readers who have asked me
to write Rosa's story over the years.

Chapter One

Summer Saturdays in a busy tourist town like Cannon Beach, Oregon, were not for the faint of heart.

As always, the sidewalk outside Rosa Galvez's gift shop, By-The-Wind, was packed with tourists. Kids in swimming suits. Parents with sunburned noses, their arms loaded with buckets and towels and umbrellas. And, her favorite, older people arm in arm, enjoying an afternoon of browsing through the local stores.

The long, wide stretch of beach that gave the town its name was only a half block from her store, which meant she had a nonstop view of the action, both in front of her store and farther down the beach.

One could never grow bored watching the kites, the recumbent bicycles, the children building sand-castles.

Some hardy souls were even swimming in the shallows, though Rosa always considered it en-tirely too cold. Maybe her childhood in Honduras had left her too warm-blooded.

Instead, she was busy working the cash regis-ter at her gift shop while her newest employee and dear friend, Jen Ryan, rearranged a display of tiny hand-carved lighthouses an artist in Lincoln City had crafted for her.

Nearby, Jen's six-year-old daughter, Addie, gig-gled at something in the small children's area Rosa had created, complete with a miniature kitchen and dollhouse. The children's area worked beautifully to keep little hands away from the more breakable items in the store while their parents browsed.

While she finished ringing up a cute handmade teapot for her customer, she kept a watchful eye on Jen. This was only her second day working in the store, though she and Addie had been in town for a few weeks. She still seemed anxious, and was constantly looking toward the door as if she expected something horrible to burst through at any moment.

Rosa hoped that with time her friend would lose

that skittish air, the impression she gave off that at the slightest provocation, she would grab her child and bolt out the door of the shop.

How could Rosa blame her, after everything Jen had been through? It was a wonder she could even go out in public. All things considered, she was doing remarkably well and seemed to be settling into life here in Cannon Beach. Having her living at Brambleberry House was a joy.

She finished carefully wrapping the customer's teapot in bubble wrap so it would be safe in whatever corner of luggage it was stuffed into.

"There you are," Rosa said, handing over the bag. "Thank you for shopping at By-The-Wind."

"Thank *you*. This is such an adorable shop. We've been to every store in town and you have the best merchandise. Authentic and charming souvenirs. I'll definitely be back before we leave town."

"I am very glad to hear this." She smiled and waved the woman and her husband on their way. She was replenishing her supply of bubble wrap under the counter when the front-door chimes rang out again.

She happened to be looking in Jen's direction and didn't miss the way her friend's features tensed with fear and then visibly relaxed when a woman came in, trailed by a young teenager.

Rosa's day, already good, immediately brightened even further, as if the sun had just come out from behind the clouds.

"Look who it is," she exclaimed. "Two of my favorite people!"

"*Hola*, Rosa," the girl said, beaming brightly at her with a mouth full of braces.

"Hello, my dear." Her friend Carrie Abbott brushed her cheek against Rosa's.

"What a wonderful surprise. How may I help you? Are you looking for a gift for someone? I have some gorgeous new purses in and also some fantastic jewelry from an artisan in Yachats you might like."

"Where's the jewelry?" Like a little magpie, Bella was instantly drawn to anything shiny.

Rosa showed her the new display and they spent a moment looking over the hand-beaded pieces.

"Ooh. Those turquoise starburst earrings are gorgeous! How much are they?"

She named an amount that had the girl's shoulders slumping. "I better not. I'm saving for an electric scooter."

"You know, that's the markup amount. I can probably drop the price by ten dollars."

Bella looked tempted. "I'm babysitting this weekend. If they're still for sale, I'll come back and get them."

"I'll set them aside until you can get back in,"

Rosa promised, which earned her another braces-filled smile.

"You're too tempting!" Carrie said, shaking her head. "I could blow my entire mad-money budget in here. Believe it or not, we didn't come in to buy earrings, no matter how lovely they are."

"Is there something else I can help you find? You should try the new soaps from Astrid Larsen."

Carrie laughed. "Stop. We're not supposed to be shopping! I came in because I need to talk to you."

Against her will, Rosa's gaze shifted to Bella and then back to the girl's mother. "Oh?" she said, hoping her voice sounded casual.

Carrie leaned against the counter. "Yes. How are you, first of all? I haven't talked to you in for-ever."

Carrie did not usually drop in just to chat. What was this about? She looked back toward Bella, who was holding the turquoise earrings up to her ears and looking in the mirror of the display.

"I have been good." She smiled. "Summer is always such a busy time here but I am glad for the tourists. Otherwise, I would not be able to keep the store open. And how are you?"

"Good. Busy, too. Bella is going in a hundred different directions, between babysitting and soft-ball and her music lessons."

Such a normal, happy childhood. It warmed her heart. "Oh, that is nice."

"Did I tell you, we have tickets to the theater in Portland next month?" Bella said. "It's a traveling Broadway production of *Hamilton*. And then we're driving down the coast to San Francisco. I cannot *wait*!"

Rosa hid a smile. Bella had only mentioned the upcoming trip about a hundred times since spring, when she and her parents had first started talking about it. "That will be wonderful for you."

"Other than that, everything is pretty good," Carrie said. "Well, okay. I do have one small problem I was hoping you might be able to help us out with."

"Of course. What can I do?"

"Don't answer so quickly. It's a huge favor."

Carrie had to know Rosa would do anything for her. Theirs was that kind of friendship.

"I was wondering if you've found a tenant to sublease your empty apartment until fall, when your renters come back."

Rosa lived on the top floor of a sprawling old Victorian, Brambleberry House. She managed the property for her aunt and her aunt's friend, Sage Benedetto Spencer.

Right now, Jen lived in the second-floor apartment, but the older couple who had been renting the furnished ground-floor apartment for the past year had moved to Texas temporarily to help with an ill family member.

"It is still empty for now."

She didn't have the energy to go the vacation-rental route, with new people constantly coming in and out.

Carrie's features brightened. "Oh, yay! Would you consider renting it for the next month or so?"

Rosa frowned. "Why would you need a place to rent? Are you doing something to your house?"

Carrie and her husband lived in a very nice cottage about a mile from Brambleberry House. She had recently remodeled the kitchen but perhaps she was thinking about doing the bathrooms.

"Not for me," Carrie assured her. "For Wyatt and Logan."

Rosa tensed at the mention of Carrie's brother and his young son. While the boy was adorable, seven years old and cheerful as could be, his father was another matter.

Wyatt Townsend was a detective for the Cannon Beach Police Department and always seemed to look at her as if she was up to something illegal.

That was surely her imagination. She had done nothing to make him suspicious of her.

"I thought he was staying with you while his home is being repaired."

"He is. And I would be fine with him living with us until the work is done, but everything is taking so much longer than he expected. It has been a nightmare of wrangling with the insurance and trying to find subcontractors to do the work."

Wyatt's small bungalow had been damaged in a fire about a month earlier, believed to have been caused by faulty wiring. It had been a small miracle that neither he nor his son had been home at the time and that a neighbor had smelled the smoke and called the fire department before widespread damage.

Rosa knew from Carrie that the fire damage still meant he had to renovate several rooms and had been living with his sister and her husband while the work was being completed.

"That must be hard for Wyatt."

"I know. And after everything they have both been through the past three years, they didn't need one more thing. But he's doing his best to rebuild."

Rosa certainly knew what it mean to rebuild a life.

"The work will take at least another month."

"That long?"

"Yes. And to be honest, I think Wyatt is a little tired of sleeping on the sofa in my family room with his leg hanging over the edge. Since the insurance company will cover rent for the next few months, he said last night he was thinking about looking around for somewhere to stay temporarily. He even brought up the idea of renting a camp trailer and parking it in his driveway until the repairs are done. I immediately thought of your empty apartment and thought that would be so much better for him and Logan, if it's still available."

The apartment was available. But did she really want Wyatt Townsend there? Rosa glanced over at Jen, who was talking to Addie in a low voice.

She could not forget about Jen. In the other woman's situation, how would she feel about having a police detective moving downstairs?

"I know it's a huge ask. You probably have a waiting list as long as my arm for an apartment in that great location."

Rosa shook her head. "I have not really put it on the market, to be honest. I have been too busy and also I know the Smiths want to move back if they can at the end of the summer, after June's mother heals from her broken hip."

That still did not mean she wanted to rent it to Wyatt and his son. She could not even say she had a compelling reason not to, other than her own unease.

The man made her so nervous. It did not help that he was extraordinarily good-looking.

He always seemed to be looking at her as if he knew she had secrets and wouldn't rest until he figured them out.

That wouldn't bother her, as she did not usually have much to do with him. Except she *did* have secrets. So many secrets. And he was the last man in town she wanted to figure them out.

She should just say no. She could tell Carrie she had decided to paint it while it was empty or put in new flooring or something.

That wasn't completely a lie. She had talked to Anna and Sage about making a few cosmetic improvements to the apartment over the summer, but had not made any solid plans. Even if she had, none of them was urgent.

The apartment was in good condition and would be an ideal solution for Wyatt and his son while repairs continued on their house.

She had to let him stay there. How could she possibly say no to Carrie? She owed her so very much.

What would Jen think? Maybe she would find comfort in knowing a big, strong police detective lived downstairs. Their own built-in security.

"Yes. Okay. He can stay there, if he wants to."

"He will," Carrie assured her, looking thrilled. "I should mention that he has a dog. He's the cutest little thing and no trouble at all."

Rosa was not so sure about that. She had seen Wyatt and Logan walking the dog on the beach a few times when she had been walking her own dog, Fiona. Their beagle mix, while adorable, seemed as energetic as Logan.

"It should be fine. The Smiths had a little dog,

too. The ground-floor apartment has a dog door out to the fenced area of the lawn. Fiona will enjoy the company."

"Oh, how perfect. It's even better than I thought. I can't thank you enough!"

"He probably will want to take a look at it before he makes any decisions. And we need to talk about rent."

She told her what the Smiths had been paying per month and Carrie's eyes widened.

"Are you kidding? That's totally a bargain around here, especially in the summer. I know the insurance company was going to pay much more than that. I'm sure it will be fantastic. You are the best."

Carrie and Bella left the store a few moments later, with Bella promising to come back so she could pay for the earrings.

As soon as the door closed behind them, Rosa slumped against the jewelry counter. What had she done?

She did *not* want Wyatt Townsend living anywhere close to her. The man looked too deeply, saw too much.

Ah, well. She would simply work a little harder to hide her secrets. She had plenty of practice.

"Sorry. Run that by me again. You did what?" Wyatt gazed at his sister in shock. She lifted her chin, somehow managing to look embarrassed and defiant at the same time. "You heard me. I talked to Rosa Galvez about you moving into her empty apartment at Brambleberry House."

He adored his older sister and owed her more than he could ever repay for the help she had given him the last three years, since Tori had died. But she had a bad habit of trying to run his life for him.

It was his own fault. He knew what Carrie was like, how she jumped on a single comment and ran with it. He should never have mentioned to her that he was thinking about renting an apartment until the fire renovations were done. He should have simply found one and told her about it later.

"When I mentioned I was thinking about moving out, I didn't mean for you to go apartment hunting right away for me."

"I know. When you said that, I remembered Rosa had an empty apartment. As far as I'm concerned, you can stay on my family-room couch forever, but I thought a three-bedroom apartment would be better than a little camp trailer for a grown man and an active seven-year-old."

Wyatt could not disagree. In truth, he had made a few inquiries himself that day, and had discovered most of the available rental homes were unavailable all summer and those that were left were out of his price range.

What else did he expect? Cannon Beach was

a popular tourist destination. Some of the short-term rentals had been booked out years in advance.

He did not mind living with his sister, brother-in-law and niece. He loved Carrie's family and Logan did, as well. But as the battle with his insurance company dragged on about doing repairs to his bungalow, he had been feeling increasingly intrusive in their lives.

Carrie was already helping him with his son. She didn't need to have them taking up every available inch of her living space with their stuff.

"The apartment at Brambleberry House is perfect! You can move in right now, it's fully furnished and available all summer."

"Why? I would have thought Rosa would want to rent it out on a longer lease."

"The couple who have been living there are supposed to be coming back in a few months. I don't think Rosa is very thrilled about having vacation renters in and out all summer."

"What makes you think having Logan and me downstairs would be better for her?"

"She knows you two. You're friends."

He was not sure he would go that far. Rosa hardly talked to him whenever they were at any kind of social event around town. He almost thought she went out of her way to avoid him, though he was not sure what he might have done to offend her.

"She said it was fine and that you can move in anytime. Today, if you want to. Isn't that wonderful?"

Again, Wyatt wasn't sure *wonderful* was the word he would use. This would only be a temporary resting place until the repairs were completed on their house.

On the other hand, it would be better for Logan than Wyatt's crazy camp-trailer idea. He couldn't deny that.

Poor kid. His world had been nothing but upheaval the past three years, though Wyatt had tried to do his best to give him a stable home life after Tori died.

Wyatt had been working as a police officer in Seattle when his wife went into cardiac arrest from a congenital heart condition none of them had known about. Logan had been four.

Numb with shock at losing his thirty-year-old, athletic, otherwise healthy wife, he had come home to Cannon Beach, where his sister lived, and taken a job with the local police department.

He hadn't known what else to do. His parents had wanted to help but both were busy professionals with demanding careers and little free time to devote to a grieving boy. Carrie had love and time in abundance, and she had urged him to move here, with a slower pace and fewer major crimes than the big city.

The move had been good for both of them. Wyatt liked his job as a detective on the Cannon Beach police force. He was busy enough that he was never bored but he was also not totally overwhelmed.

He worked on a couple of drug task forces and the SWAT team, which had only been called out a handful of times during his tenure here, all for domestic situations.

The move had been even better for Logan. He loved spending time with his aunt, uncle and older cousin, Bella. He had a wide circle of friends and a budding interest in marine biology.

Wyatt loved seeing his son thrive and knew Carrie and her family were a huge part of that. Logan spent as much time at her house as he did their own.

During the past month, both of them had spent more than enough time with Carrie and her family, since they were living there.

Another month and they could move back to his house, he hoped.

Wyatt counted his blessings that his bungalow hadn't been a complete loss. Fire crews had responded quickly and had been able to save most of the house except the kitchen, where the fire had started, probably from old, faulty wiring. The main living area had also been burned. Even so, all the rooms had suffered water and smoke damage.

Dealing with the renovations was a tedious job, filled with paperwork, phone calls and aggravation, but Wyatt could definitely see the light at the end of the tunnel.

"What do you think?" Carrie looked apprehensive but excited. "Don't you think it's a fabulous idea? Brambleberry House is so close, you can easily drop off Logan when you need me to watch him."

Location definitely was a plus. Carrie's house and Rosa's were only a few blocks apart. Brambleberry House was also positioned about halfway between his house and his sister's, which would be convenient when he was overseeing the repairs.

Wyatt knew there were many advantages to moving into an apartment at Brambleberry House. Wouldn't it be good to have their own space again? Somewhere he could walk around in his underwear once in a while if he needed to grab a pair of jeans out of the dryer, without having to worry about his sister or his niece walking in on him?

"It could work," he said, not quite willing to jump a hundred percent behind the idea. "Are you sure Rosa is okay with it?"

"Totally great." Carrie gave a bright smile that somehow had a tinge of falseness to it. What wasn't she telling him? Did Rosa Galvez really want to rent the apartment or had Carrie somehow manipulated her into doing it?

He wouldn't put it past his sister. She had a way of persuading people to her way of thinking.

Wyatt's cop instincts told him there was more to Rosa Galvez than one could see on the surface. She had secrets, but then most people did.

The bottom line was, he was not interested in digging into her secrets. She could keep them.

As long as she obeyed the law, he was not going to pry into her business. Rosa could have all the secrets she wanted. It was nothing to him.

So why, then, was he so apprehensive about moving into Brambleberry House?

He did not have a rational reason to say no. It really did make sense to have their own place. It would be better for Logan, which was the only thing that mattered, really.

It was only a month, maybe two at the most. Wyatt would survive his unease around her.

"Are you sure the apartment is affordable?"

"Absolutely. She told me how much she's charging and you won't find anything else nearly as nice in that price range. It's well within your budget. And I forgot to mention, the apartment already has a dog door for Hank and a fenced area in the yard."

That would be another plus. Logan's beagle mix was gregarious, energetic and usually adorable, but Carrie's two ragdoll cats were not fans of the dog. They would be more than glad to have Hank out of their territory.

"It sounds ideal," he said, finally surrendering to the inevitable. "Thanks for looking into it for us."

"As I said, the apartment is ready immediately. You can stay there tonight, if you want."

He blinked. How had things progressed so quickly from him merely mentioning the night before that he was thinking about moving out to his sister handling all the details and basically shoving him out the door today?

He could think of no good reason to wait and forced a smile. "Great. I'll start packing everything up and we can head over as soon as Logan gets home from day camp."

Carrie's face lit up. "You can at least wait for dinner. I imagine Rosa is probably working until six or seven, anyway."

"Right."

"I think you're going to love it. Rosa is so nice and she has a new tenant, Jen Ryan, who has a little girl who is a bit younger than Logan. Rosa has a wonderful dog, Fiona, who is more human than dog, if you ask me. I'm sure Hank will love her."

At the sound of his name, Wyatt's beagle mix jumped up from the floor, grabbed a ball and plopped it at Wyatt's feet. He picked it up and tossed it down the hall. Hank scrambled after it, much to the disdain of one of the ragdolls, who was sprawled out in a patch of sunlight.

He had seen Rosa on the beach, walking a gorgeous Irish setter. They were hard to miss, the lovely woman and her elegant dog.

Rosa was hard to miss anywhere. She was the sort of woman who drew attention, only in part because of her beautiful features and warm dark eyes.

She exuded warmth and friendliness, at least with everyone else in town. With Wyatt, she seemed watchful and reserved.

That didn't matter, he supposed. She was kind enough to let him live in her apartment for the next month. He didn't need her to be his best friend.

Chapter Two

Now that the deed was done, Rosa was having second, third and fourth thoughts about Wyatt Townsend moving in downstairs.

Why had she ever thought this would work?

That evening as she pulled weeds in the backyard after leaving the store, she had to fight all her instincts that were urging her to call up Carrie right now and tell her she had made a mistake. The apartment was no longer available.

"There is no law against changing your mind, is there?" she asked out loud to Fiona, who was lying in the grass nearby, watching butterflies dance amid the climbing roses.

The dog gave her a curious look then turned back to her business, leaving Rosa to sigh. She yanked harder at a stubborn weed that had driven deep roots into the ground.

She would do nothing. She had given her word and could not back out now. Integrity, keeping her word, was important. She had learned that first from her own mother and then from her adopted parents.

Lauren and Daniel Galvez were two of the most honorable people she knew. They would never think of reneging on a promise and she couldn't, either.

Yes, Wyatt made her extremely nervous. She did not want him moving in downstairs. But she had given her word to his sister. End of story.

Because of that, she would be gracious and welcoming to him and to his sweet son.

Thinking about Logan left her feeling a little bit better about the decision. He was a very adorable boy, with good manners and a ready smile.

It was not the boy's fault that Wyatt made her so nervous.

She had almost talked herself into at least accepting the new status quo, when an SUV pulled up to the house a half hour later.

Fiona lifted her head to sniff the air, then rose and hurried over to the vehicle to greet the newcomers.

Rosa climbed to her feet a little more slowly, pulled off her gloves and swiped at her hair before she headed for the vehicle. She might be accepting of her new tenants, but summoning the same kind of enthusiasm her dog showed so readily would be a stretch.

When Rosa reached the vehicle, Logan was opening the back door and jumping to the ground, his little dog close behind.

Fiona barked a greeting, then leaned in to sniff the newcomer, tail wagging. The Townsends' dog sniffed back, and a moment later, the two were circling each other with joy.

At least Fiona was happy to have them here.

"Hello, Logan," Rosa said.

"Hi." The boy beamed at her, showing off a gap in his teeth that she found adorable.

"Guess what?" he said. "We're moving into your house! Dad says we can stay here until our house is done and I'll have my own bedroom and won't have to sleep in Aunt Carrie's sewing room anymore."

"This is so wonderful, no?" She smiled down at him, trying not to pay any attention to his father walking around the vehicle, looking big and serious and intimidating.

"What is the name of your dog?"

"This is Hank. Don't worry. He's nice."

"I never doubted it for a minute," she assured him. "Hello, Hank."

She reached down to pet the dog, who responded by rolling over to have his belly scratched. Rosa loved him immediately.

"This is Fiona. She is also very nice."

Logan grinned and petted Fiona's long red coat.

Wouldn't it be lovely if she only had to deal with the boy and the dog? Unfortunately, the boy had a father. She had to say something to Wyatt, at least. Bracing herself, she lifted her attention from the two dogs and the boy, and faced the man who always looked as if he could see through her skin and bones into her heart, and was not convinced he liked what he saw.

She drew in a deep breath and forced a smile. "Hello. Welcome to Brambleberry House."

He nodded, always so serious. "Thank you for allowing us to stay here until our house is repaired. It's very kind of you."

She shrugged. "The apartment was empty. Houses are meant to be lived in. Brambleberry House in particular seems a little sad without people, especially children."

She immediately regretted her words, especially when Wyatt raised a skeptical eyebrow.

"Your house seems sad."

Logan giggled. "Houses can't be sad. They're just houses."

She shrugged. "This is no ordinary house. I think you will find that after you have been here a few nights. Come. I will show you your apartment."

She did not wait for a response, but simply walked up the front steps and into the entryway.

"There are three levels of the house with three apartments, one taking up each level. We share the foyer. We try to keep the outside door locked for the security of our residents. I will give you the code, as well as the key."

She was even more vigilant about that right now for Jen's sake.

Wyatt nodded. "Makes sense."

"Your apartment has a separate key. It is on the ground floor. I live on the top floor. If you have any questions or problems, you can find me there or at the store."

"My sister told me you have another new tenant on the second floor."

Rosa's protective instincts flared. "This is true. Her name is Jen Ryan. She lives there with her daughter, Addie, who is six."

"I don't believe I know her."

It was one thing for Wyatt to look at *her* with suspicion. She could not let him turn his police detective's scrutiny toward Jen.

"Jen and Addie only moved here a short time

ago from Utah. She is a friend of mine from university."

"Ah. That must be why her name doesn't ring a bell. What brought her to Cannon Beach?"

Rosa's hackles rose. Jen did not need all these questions. It would not do for Wyatt to become too curious. "She works for me. She was looking for a change and I needed someone to help me at the gift store."

He nodded. "Guess I haven't been in for a while or I might have met her already."

He hadn't been in ever, as far as she could remember. But then, Wyatt Townsend was not the sort to buy shell wind chimes or lighthouse-shaped knickknacks.

"I can introduce you after I show you your apartment, if you would like."

"Sure."

Better to get their introduction out of the way. With luck, Wyatt could then forget about Jen.

She would have to send a text to Jen to warn her before showing up at her door with a police detective.

She had already told the other woman about the new tenant moving in. As she had expected, Jen had been both apprehensive and relieved, for a complex mix of reasons.

"This house is big," Logan exclaimed, looking

up at the grand entry stairway, one of Rosa's favorite parts of Brambleberry House.

She smiled, in full agreement. "Yes. Each apartment has at least two bedrooms and two bathrooms. And each has a lovely view of the ocean."

She unlocked the first-floor apartment and swung open the door. Immediately, the sweet scent of freesia drifted through the air.

It wasn't unusual to smell flowers at random places in the house. She knew her aunt Anna and Sage Spencer believed the ghost of the previous owner still walked the halls.

Abigail Dandridge had died a decade ago and left the house jointly to Anna and Sage. She had been dear friends to them and also had left Anna By-The-Wind, the gift shop in town that Rosa was a part owner of and now running.

All the old-timers in town still remembered Abigail with fondness. Hardly a week went by when someone did not come into the shop with a memory of Abigail.

Rosa wished she could have known her. She also wanted to be the sort of person whom people remembered with such fondness.

She wasn't sure she believed the stories that Abigail still lingered in the home she had loved and she was also quite certain a no-nonsense police officer like Wyatt Townsend would never believe a benevolent spirit drifted through the place.

She couldn't deny that scent of freesia, though, which had no logical explanation.

Ignoring it for now, she let them inside the apartment.

"This apartment is the largest in the house. It has three bedrooms and a very nice sunroom. The master bedroom and the kitchen face the ocean. The other two bedrooms each have a view of the garden."

"Oh, I like this place." Logan ran into the sunroom, which had an entire wall made of glass.

"That looks like a great place to read a book on a stormy afternoon."

"Yeah. Maybe you can read me more of *The Hobbit*," Logan said.

"Sure thing."

Wyatt smiled down at his son with a softness Rosa had not seen before. Instead of looking stern and foreboding, he looked younger and far more handsome.

A little shiver of awareness blossomed in her stomach. She swallowed, taken completely off guard.

No. No, no, *no*. She did not want to be attracted to this man. It was nothing personal against Wyatt Townsend. She wasn't interested in romance at all. Okay, it was a *little* personal. She especially didn't want to suddenly find herself attracted to a police detective who was trained to be suspicious of people.

She let out a slow breath. This was ridiculous. He was her tenant and her friend's brother. That was all. She was not attracted to him. She would simply not allow it.

She had too much to worry about right now, keeping Jen safe. She did not have time to be distracted by a gruff detective, no matter how sweetly he smiled at his adorable son.

"The laundry room is off the kitchen there. You can control the temperature of your apartment independently of the other two units in the house. The control is in the hallway. The garbage trucks, they come on Monday. This apartment has a dog door so that Hank can go out into the fenced area of the yard during the day if he needs."

"That will be handy."

"The garden is for all the guests to use at any time. We have a swing in the tree that Logan might enjoy. I know that Addie does. We also have direct access to the beach, but I ask that you keep the gate locked for security reasons. It is the same code as the front door, which I have written on the paper for you, and your key will also open it."

"Got it."

"Do you have any questions?"

"I have a question," Logan said. "Can Hank and me play with your dog sometime?"

She smiled. "Of course. Anytime. She comes to the store with me most of the time during the day, but when we are home, she would love to play with you."

She looked up to find Wyatt watching her with an expression she could not read. It still made her nervous.

"If you think of any other questions, my phone number is there on the desk."

"Got it. Thank you again. We'll try not to be any trouble for you."

His features were stern once more, making her wish suddenly that he would smile at her as he smiled at his son.

"Yes. We don't like trouble here at Bramble-berry House. I would hate to have to call the *policia* on you."

Logan's eyes went big. "My dad is the *policia*!"

She smiled at him. "I know. I was only teasing. Do you have things I could help you carry in?"

"Not much. A couple of suitcases. Logan and I can get them."

"Only that?"

"We're traveling pretty light these days. A lot of our things were damaged in the fire by the smoke and by the water from the fire hoses."

She needed the reminder that they had been through difficult things the past few months. It was a small sacrifice to offer a home to them, which she could easily do.

She could also be kind and gracious to them, despite her personal misgivings about having Wyatt in her space.

"I am sorry for that. If there is anything else you need, please let me know."

"Carrie said you have dishes and pots and pans and things."

"Yes. The apartment is fully furnished."

"That will be handy. Thanks."

His poor little boy. First, he lost his mother, then he lost his house to a fire. She wanted to cuddle him close and make everything all better.

"What about food? You will need to get groceries."

"Carrie sent along some meals I only have to thaw and heat for the first few days. We'll head to the grocery store this evening to pick up some staples after we unload our things. Most of the time, we eat pretty simply, don't we, Logan?"

The boy nodded. "Except Aunt Carrie says we go out to eat too much and I need more vegetables." He gave Rosa a conspiratorial look. "I don't really like vegetables."

"Yes, but you must eat them, anyway, if you want to be strong and healthy when you grow up. My mother used to tell me 'Rosa, if you eat enough vegetables, soon they will taste like candy.' They never did, but I still like vegetables."

He laughed, as she'd hoped, and Rosa felt a little pang. She loved children but didn't expect she would ever have any of her own, for a wide variety of reasons.

"Your mother sounds funny."

"She was. She always tried to make me laugh, even when things sometimes felt very dark."

She missed her mother deeply. The older she got, the more Rosa realized how many sacrifices Maria Elena made on her behalf. She had never been hungry, even though she knew her mother barely made a living cleaning homes for some of the more well-off people in their village. Her mother had always insisted she work hard at school so she could have a brighter future.

She pushed away the memories of her childhood. Her first fifteen years sometimes seemed a lifetime ago, as if they had happened to someone else.

"Oh," she said, suddenly remembering. "I wanted you to meet Jen and Addie, who live upstairs from you."

"All right."

"Let me check if she can meet you."

She quickly sent a text to her friend. After a longer-than-usual pause, Jen replied that she and Addie would come down to the foyer.

"She said she would meet us outside your door," she explained to Wyatt.

"Okay."

"You will like Addie, Logan. Maybe you will make a new friend."

"Maybe."

Life could be filled with so much pain sometimes, Rosa thought as they walked out into the hall to wait for Jen. Each of the inhabitants of Brambleberry House had walked a hard road.

At least for now, they had a safe place to rest, a beautiful home set on the seashore surrounded by flowers, one that might contain a friendly spirit who could not seem to leave.

As Wyatt waited for his upstairs neighbor to come down to meet him and Logan, he couldn't shake the feeling that this was too good to be true.

The apartment was perfect for their needs, with a good-size bedroom for Logan and a very nice en suite for him, as well as an extra room he could use for an office if he needed.

It was actually bigger than their little house and certainly had a bigger yard for Logan to play in.

Brambleberry House would be an ideal temporary home for them while the construction crew repaired the fire damage at his place.

He still had misgivings but Rosa had been welcoming enough. She was certainly kind to Logan, if still distant toward Wyatt.

He followed her into the foyer, with its sweeping staircase and elegant chandelier, to find a woman walking down with a young girl's hand clutched tightly in hers.

She had brown hair pulled back into a tight ponytail and quite striking blue eyes with shadows under them.

"Jen, here are the new tenants I was telling you about," Rosa said in her melodious, accented voice. "This is Wyatt Townsend and his son, Logan. Wyatt is a police officer in Cannon Beach and Logan is seven years old, starting second grade when the summer is over."

"Hello."

She was soft-spoken and didn't meet his gaze directly.

Just what he needed. Another woman here who had secrets.

"Pleasure to meet you." He purposely kept his voice calm, neutral, as he did when he walked into a situation where a witness or a suspect might be prone to bolt.

He didn't miss the way Rosa placed her body slightly in front of her friend's, as if to protect her. He had a feeling Jen didn't miss it, either.

From him? Did Rosa really think he posed a threat to either of them?

The little girl seemed to have none of her mother's skittishness. She stepped forward with a big smile. "Hi. My name is Addie and I'm six years old."

"Hi, Addie." Wyatt was happy to see she seemed well-adjusted and friendly. Whatever was going on with her mother hadn't impacted her yet.

"Hi," she said to Logan, who hadn't said anything yet. "My name is Addie."

"I know. I heard you before."

"What's your name?"

"Logan. I'm seven." His son spoke with a tinge of superiority over his advanced age that made Wyatt hide a smile.

He caught Rosa's gaze and didn't miss her surprised look. What? Did she think he never smiled?

Addie pointed behind them. "Is that your dog?"

Wyatt turned to find Hank plopped in the doorway as if he owned the place.

"Yep," Logan answered. "His name is Hank."

"Will he bite?"

"Only if you bite him first," Logan said, which made Addie giggle.

"I'm not going to bite a dog! That would be gross."

"You can pet him, if you want."

She plopped onto the ground and Hank, predictably, rolled over to have his belly scratched. The dog was shameless for affection.

"I don't have a dog, I have a cat. Her name is Lucy. She's old," Addie explained. "Sometimes I pretend that Fi is my dog."

"Who is Fi?" Logan looked confused.

"Fiona," Rosa explained. "My dog, remember? Sometimes we call her Fi. And you can pretend all you want, darling."

"I will," the girl said cheerfully.

"How are you enjoying Cannon Beach so far?" Wyatt asked Jen Ryan.

She focused her attention somewhere over his shoulder, still not meeting his gaze.

"I like it here. The people are friendly, for the most part, and the scenery is amazing."

"Rosa said you came from Utah. I've got friends there. What part?"

He wasn't surprised when his innocent-seeming question made both Rosa and Jen tense. As he suspected, she was in some kind of trouble. Was she running from an abusive relationship or a custody problem? Or something else?

The two women looked at each other for a moment then Jen gave a smile that looked forced. "A small town in Utah, near the Idaho border. No one has ever heard of it."

She answered in such an offhand manner, he knew she was being deliberately evasive.

He wanted to ask her what town in Utah, but suspected she would shut down fast if he asked.

He also didn't want to raise the wrath of Rosa Galvez. Not when she was doing him a big favor by letting him stay here.

Anyway, Jen Ryan was only a neighbor. Not a suspect.

She probably had very legit reasons to be cautious of strangers.

Sometimes he needed to remind himself to separate the detective from the man. They would be sharing this house for the next month, but likely would not see much of each other, anyway. Did he really need to know the poor woman's life story?

"Rosa says you are a police detective."

"Yes."

"I see."

She didn't sound thrilled at the confirmation. He couldn't help feeling a little defensive. He was passionate about his job, protecting and serving, and tried to do it with compassion and dedication toward all.

"It was nice to meet you," she said, though he suspected she was lying. "I hope you're comfortable here."

"Thank you."

"Come on, Addie."

The girl protested a little but still took her mother's hand and the two of them went back up the stairs again. Addie sent a smile over her shoulder all the way up the stairs at Logan and Hank and her pretend dog, Fiona.

That one would be a little heartbreaker when she grew up. He could tell she already knew how to charm people.

He turned back to Rosa in time to see her watching Jen with a worried expression. When she felt his gaze, she quickly wiped it away.

"There. Now everyone knows everyone else living in the house."

"Yes." One big not-so-happy family. "We'll just grab our things and settle in."

She nodded. "Be sure to contact me if you have any questions."

"Thank you."

"Good night, then. Come on, Fiona. We have tools to put away."

She walked outside in the fading sunlight and he and Logan followed her to grab their suitcases and the few boxes of belongings he had brought from his sister's house.

When they returned from the last trip outside, Logan collapsed onto the comfortable-looking couch. "I like this place. It feels nice."

Logan was the reason he was here. Wyatt was grateful for the reminder. He and his son needed their own place until the house was ready. It was only a short time, and then they could get back to their real life.

Yes, he might be uncomfortably attracted to Rosa Galvez, but he wasn't about to make the mistake of acting on that attraction.

No matter how tempting.

Chapter Three

The busy summer season and her responsibilities at By-The-Wind, combined with her volunteer activities, meant Rosa only saw her new tenants in passing for several days after they moved in.

Even when she didn't actively see them, she was aware of them. Knowing that Wyatt was living two floors below her, she couldn't seem to stop imagining him walking around the house at night. Taking a shower, sprawling out on the big king-size bed wearing next to nothing...

Her entirely too vivid imagination annoyed her severely. When she would catch her mind dwelling on him, she would quickly jerk away her attention and make herself think about something boring, like taking inventory or meeting with her tax accountant. Anything to keep her mind off the attractive man who lived downstairs.

She wasn't sure how she would make it through an entire month or more of this.

Rosa was trying hard to remember that Wyatt and Logan were guests in the house. A month wasn't long, especially during the busy tourist season, when the store was so busy she didn't have much free time, anyway.

She could endure having them there, even if their stay dragged into two months, especially as it was one small way she could work on repaying her vast debt to his sister.

Nearly a week after Wyatt and Logan moved in, Rosa sat in her spare bedroom at the desk she had pulled beneath the window overlooking the Pacific, wishing for rain. For the last few days, the weather seemed as unsettled as she felt. The days had been overcast, brooding like a petulant teenager.

Outside, the ocean seethed and churned, restless in the random moonbeams that found their way through the gathering clouds.

Perhaps a storm would blow through and wash away the unseasonable heat that seemed to have settled over the area.

Brambleberry House did not have air conditioning, as summers here along the coast were mild. The nights usually turned cooler, but until the sun went down, her apartment on the third floor of the old house could be stultifying.

Rosa spent most of her evenings working in the garden. She missed Sonia Davis, the woman who had lived on the second floor until two Christmases earlier, when her estranged husband had come to fetch her, and Rosa had learned her tenant had been living under an assumed name.

Rosa's thumb wasn't nearly as green as Sonia's, and her friend now lived happily with her husband in Haven Point, Idaho. The gardens didn't look as good as they had under Sonia's care, but Rosa did her best.

To her delight, Jen and Addie joined her most evenings. She enjoyed both the company and the help, and was thrilled to see Jen becoming more at ease here in Cannon Beach.

Her friend was settling in. She seemed more comfortable at the gift shop, as well, no longer looking as if she wanted to escape every time a man walked in.

Rosa felt good about her progress. She had wondered if encouraging Jen and her daughter to leave behind their life in Utah was the best decision. Seeing her friend begin to relax into her new life gave her hope that she had been right.

Rain suddenly clicked against the window and

she looked up from her laptop. Finally! Perhaps a storm would at last blow away the heat.

Unable to resist, she opened the window more and leaned down to watch the storm roll in.

Lightning arced across the sky, followed closely by a low rumble of thunder. In the blast of light, she could see the sea, dark and tumultuous.

Rosa loved a good storm. They probably should frighten her, especially after some of the intense storms she had experienced in Honduras, but she always found them invigorating. Refreshing in their own way.

She gave up work and decided to relax with a book. The only thing better than a storm was curling up with a good book while she enjoyed it from a safe shelter.

Books had saved her when she first came to the United States. She had always loved to read, but the book selection had been limited in their village.

Once she had moved in with Daniel and Lauren, she had free rein at the town library in Moose Springs and at the school library. Books helped her learn English. Like most other girls her age, she had fallen in love with Harry Potter. Lauren had been wise enough to buy her both the Spanish and the English versions. Rosa would read both at the same time, comparing the words and the sentences to help with her word fluency and her grammar construction.

She still reread the books often. Once in a while she would read the Spanish version so that she didn't lose touch with the language of her heart, but mostly she read in English.

She was currently reading a cozy mystery by one of her favorite authors. She settled into her favorite reading spot, a wide armchair in the corner of her bedroom, and was deep into the story when she was distracted by a sudden banging from outside.

The sound stopped as abruptly as it started. She sank back down and picked up her book again, then she heard it once more.

With a sigh, she set aside the book. If only she had a landlord she could call. Unfortunately, things that banged in the night were *her* responsibility.

She had a feeling she knew what the trouble was. The door on the garden shed wasn't latching tightly. She had noticed it the last time she had mowed the lawn.

If she wasn't mistaken, that was the door to the shed blowing open, then banging shut.

Lightning flashed again, and in that burst of light, she could see she was right. The garden shed door was wide open.

As much as she didn't want to go out into the rain, she couldn't let the banging continue all night, for her tenants' sake, as well as to protect the contents of the shed.

Rosa threw on her rain boots and coat and found a flashlight, then hurried down the stairs.

When she reached the bottom step, the door to the ground-floor apartment swung open suddenly. Startled, she almost stumbled but caught herself just in time.

Wyatt stood there, silhouetted by the light coming from inside the apartment. He looked rumbled and gorgeous, his hair messy as if he had been dozing.

He was wearing jeans and a T-shirt, and was barefoot. Through the open doorway, she could see a television on inside with a baseball game playing.

Logan was nowhere in sight, which led her to believe he must be sleeping.

Her mouth felt dry suddenly and Rosa had to grip the railing of the stairs to keep her balance.

Ridiculous. What was *wrong* with her?

"Sounds like trouble out there."

She nodded. "Nothing major. I believe it is the door to the garden shed. It is not latching the way it should."

"You're not going out in that, are you? Some of those lightning strikes seem close. That's nothing to mess around with."

"I know. But I cannot let it bang all night to disturb everyone."

He gave her a long look, then nodded. "Give

me a moment to throw on some shoes, then I'll come with you."

"That is not necessary," she protested. "I can wedge it closed with a rock if I can't fix it."

"Wait. I'll only be a minute."

She really could handle it by herself, but didn't want to be rude so she waited. A few moments later, he returned wearing tennis shoes and a raincoat with a Cannon Beach Police Department logo.

Together they walked out of the house. The temperature had cooled down considerably. Rosa shivered a little at the wet wind that blew through the porch.

Her eagle-eyed neighbor didn't miss her reaction. "I can handle this, if you want to stay here on the porch, where it's dry."

She shook her head. "*You* should stay here where it's dry. Taking care of the house is my responsibility."

"Fine. We'll both go."

She pulled up her hood and hurried down the steps toward the garden shed.

When they reached it, she was grateful for his help. The door was heavy and the wind made it hard to move. She wasn't sure she could have wrestled it on her own.

"I don't think you're going to be able to fix the latch tonight. Where's the rock you were talking about so we can keep it closed until the weather is a little better?"

"I will have to find something."

Lightning flashed again, followed almost immediately by thunder. It was one thing to enjoy the storm from the comfort of her easy chair. It was something else to be out in the middle of it, with the wind whipping raindrops hard at her face.

She fumbled to turn on the light inside the shed. Wyatt joined her in the small space and she was instantly aware of him. He smelled delicious, some sort of masculine scent that reminded her of the mountains around Moose Gulch, covered in sagebrush and pine.

His gaze landed on a heavy concrete block. "That should do it for now."

He reached down to pick it up and brushed against her. Rosa quickly took a step back, though there wasn't much room to escape.

He didn't appear to notice, much to her relief.

He left the shed again. She took a moment to draw a steadying breath, then turned to follow him. As she reached to turn the light off, her hand caught on something sharp inside.

Pain sliced through her and she couldn't help her gasp.

"What is it?"

"Nothing," she said. "Only a scratch. I am fine."

In another lightning flash, she saw he looked doubtful but he didn't argue with her.

He muscled the door shut, then wedged the concrete block in front of it.

"That should do it, barring a hurricane tonight." He raised his voice to be heard over the storm.

"Let us hope we do not have a hurricane. I had enough of those when I was a girl."

He gave her an interested look but didn't ask questions. Another lightning bolt lit up the sky, followed by the loudest thunder yet, a rumble that seemed to shake the little garden shed.

"That one was too close." Wyatt frowned. "We need to get to shelter. We're too exposed here."

He led the way to the closest entry to the house, the door to his sunroom.

This was one of her favorite parts about Brambleberry House. If she was ever tempted to leave her third-floor sanctuary, it would be to move to this floor so that she could have the sunroom, with the glorious view of the ocean.

Rosa could spend all day every day here. She would probably put in a bed so she could sleep here on long summer nights with the sound of the sea and the breeze blowing through.

She liked the idea of it but the reality probably would not be as appealing. She would feel too exposed here. Anyone could walk up from the beach, climb over the beach gate and break a window to get in.

She would have no defenses.

That was the reason she had not given this apartment to Jen, though both had come vacant at the same time and this apartment was larger. Jen needed to feel safe, above all else.

Security wasn't an issue for Wyatt. Something told Rosa the man could take care of himself in all situations.

"Now," he said when they were inside, "let's take a look at your hand."

Rosa tensed, suddenly aware of how cozy this sunroom was in the middle of a storm.

She should not have come in here with him. Not when she was fighting this unwanted attraction.

"It is fine. I only need to put a bandage on it. I can take care of it upstairs."

Wyatt frowned. "It's your right hand, which is always harder to bandage for someone who is right-handed. Let me take a look."

How had he noticed she was right-handed? Something told her Wyatt was a man who did not miss much.

He flipped on the light inside the sunroom and held out his hand. Unless she wanted to run through the apartment and up two flights of stairs in her awkward rain boots, she had no choice but to show him the wound.

The cut on her palm was about two inches long, shallow but bloody.

Rosa felt her knees go weak at the sight of those streaks of red. To her great embarrassment, the sight of blood always left her feeling as if she would faint.

Her mother used to be a healer of sorts and people would come to their small house for care. Maria Elena had even delivered a few babies.

Rosa had never liked seeing blood or having to help her mother clean it up. It was a weakness she despised in herself, but one she couldn't seem to help.

"Sit down and I'll go grab my first-aid kit. Normally, I keep one in the kitchen but it burned up in the fire. Lucky for you, I've got another one out in my vehicle."

Was she lucky? Rosa would have liked to argue but she was trying too hard not to look at the blood dripping off her hand.

After he left, she tried to focus instead on the storm still rumbling around them.

He and Logan had already left a mark on this room. It was obviously well-used. A couple of children's chapter books were stacked on the table and she could see some small trucks on the floor.

Wyatt returned a moment later with a red case. "Come into the kitchen, where we can wash off the blood. I should have had you do that while I was getting the first-aid kit. Sorry. I wasn't thinking."

She followed him, trying to come up with the words to tell him again that she could take care of her very minor injury on her own.

No words would come to her other than the truth—that she was afraid to let him touch her.

Since she couldn't tell him that, of course, she followed him into the kitchen.

Here, again, he and Logan had made the space their own. A couple of art-class projects had been stuck with magnets to the refrigerator and homework was spread out on the table.

Hank, his cute little dog, wandered into the room and stretched in a dog-yoga pose as Wyatt pulled a few paper towels off the roll.

"Come over here by the sink."

Keeping her gaze fixed away from the cut, she followed him. He turned on the sink and ran his hand under it for a few moments to gauge the temperature, then carefully gripped her hand and guided it under.

Rosa held her breath. Why did he have to smell so good?

He turned her hand this way and that to rinse off the blood. "I don't think you need stitches. It's fairly shallow."

"That is what I thought also."

"We can clean it off pretty well and I think I have a bandage big enough to cover it."

She didn't see any point in arguing with him when he was trying to help her. "Thank you."

Why did her voice sound so breathy and soft? She had to hope he did not notice.

Lightning flashed again outside, followed almost immediately by a loud clap of thunder. She managed to swallow her instinctive gasp.

"How does Logan sleep through such a noise?"

He smiled softly and she felt those nerves sizzle inside her again.

"He can sleep through just about anything. It's a talent I wish I shared."

"I, as well." She was unable to resist smiling back. He seemed a different person when talking about his son, much more open and approachable.

He looked at her for a moment, then seemed to jerk his attention back to her hand.

He patted it dry with a bit of gauze from the first-aid kit. "I didn't see what you scratched your hand on out there."

"A nail, I think. I am not sure. I will have to look more closely in the daylight."

He nodded. "Any idea when your last tetanus shot was? If it was a nail, it might be rusty. This is the coast, after all. Everything rusts."

"I had the shot only a few years ago after I

stepped on a rock at the beach and needed a few stitches."

It was a good thing she had been with friends that time. Her foot had bled so much, she probably would have been too light-headed to walk to her car.

"Good news, then. You shouldn't need a second shot. I'm just going to put a little first-aid cream on it. If it doesn't start to heal in a few days, you will probably want to see your doctor."

"Yes. I will do that."

She missed having Melissa Fielding living in this apartment. Melissa was a nurse and was great at patching up scrapes and cuts. Now she was happily married to Eli Sanderson, who was a doctor in town. Eli was a wonderful stepfather to Melissa's daughter, Skye, and they had a new baby of their own, Thomas.

Wyatt squeezed out the antibiotic cream on the bandage before sticking it onto her skin.

"That is smart."

"A little trick my mother taught me."

"She sounds like a very wise woman."

He smiled a little and she again had to order her nerves to behave. "She is. She's a judge in Portland. That's where Carrie and I grew up."

"I thought your mother was friends with Abigail." She frowned a little, trying to make the connection.

"She was, sort of. It was really our grandmother who was best friends with Abigail. My mother grew up here, in a house not far from Brambleberry House. Her parents lived there until they died several years ago. I can remember visiting Abigail a few times, back in the days when the house was all one unit, with no apartments."

The curtains suddenly fluttered and Hank, who had just settled down on the kitchen rug, rose again to sniff at the air. Rosa could swear she suddenly smelled freesia.

"Do you smell that?"

He sniffed. "What?"

"Flowers."

He raised an eyebrow. "I smell vanilla and berries. It's making me hungry."

She could feel herself flush and was grateful he probably could not tell with her brown skin. That was her shampoo, probably.

"I thought I smelled freesia. That was Abigail's signature scent."

"Why would it still smell like her?"

"My aunt and her friend who own the house think Abigail still wanders through the house. Do not worry. If she is here, she is a kind spirit, I think."

"Do you buy that?"

"Not really. Sometimes I must wonder, though."

He seemed to take the news of a ghost in stride.

"I suppose I'm a big skeptic. I haven't noticed anything in the time we've been living here."

"Did you not see Hank standing in the corner, looking at nothing? Fiona sometimes does that. She makes me wonder what she can see that I cannot."

"I hadn't really noticed."

She studied him. "Would you mind if Abigail were still hanging about?"

"Not really. I remember her as being very kind when I was a boy. She always gave me butterscotch candy."

He smiled a little at the memory.

"As long as she doesn't watch me while I sleep, we should get along fine."

Rosa had a hard enough time not thinking about him sleeping a few floors below her. She didn't need another reason to picture it.

"I do not know if you can tell a ghost she is not welcome in your bedroom."

He smiled. It wasn't a huge smile and certainly not anything as overt as laughter. She still found it enormously appealing.

She wanted to stare at his mouth, will his lips to lift again into a smile as heat soaked through her.

After an awkward moment, she forced herself to look away. She slid her hand back and pressed it into her stomach against the silly butterflies dancing there.

"I should go," she said. "Thank you for your help with the door and with this."

She raised her hand and, as if she had waved a magic wand, another bolt of lightning lit up the kitchen and an instant later the lights flickered and went out.

"Oh, dear," she exclaimed. "I was afraid of this happening."

"It would not be a storm along the coast without some kind of power outage."

He went to the window of the living area that faced out to the street. "I don't see any lights on in the whole neighborhood. It looks like the power is out everywhere."

Rosa knew that was not unusual. Electricity often went out during big storms in the area.

She knew there was nothing to fear. Still, she could feel herself begin to panic. Full darkness always did that to her. It reminded her too much of hiding in the back of a pickup truck, afraid she would not see another day.

"Where is my flashlight? Did I leave it in your sunroom?" She looked around the dark kitchen, as if she could summon it with her will, and tried not to panic.

He must have sensed some of her unease. Wyatt reached out a comforting hand and rested it briefly on her arm. Heat radiated from where he touched her and she wanted to lean into his warmth and solid strength.

"I'll find it. Stay here. I don't want you to hurt yourself again."

She leaned against the kitchen sink, breathing deeply and ordering herself to be calm.

A moment later, he returned with her flashlight on, pointed to the ground so he didn't shine it in her eyes.

"Here you are."

"Thank you."

She felt silly at her overreaction, wishing for a different past that wasn't filled with moments of fear and pain.

"Thank you again for your help. Good night."

She turned to leave and somehow wasn't surprised when he followed closely behind her.

"I'll walk you up the stairs to your place."

She shook her head slightly. "That is really not necessary. I can find my way. I am up and down these stairs all the time."

"Maybe so. But not in the dark. I would hate for you to fall on my watch."

She didn't want to argue with him. Not when he was being so helpful. She gave an inward sigh as she headed for the apartment door and out to the main foyer.

Wyatt followed her up one flight of stairs. When she saw Jen's door, Rosa immediately felt guilty.

She had been so busy trying not to become stupid over Wyatt Townsend, she had not given a thought to her friend and how nervous Jen and Addie might be in the dark.

She was a terrible friend. The worst.

She paused outside the door and turned to face him. "I should probably check on Jen and Addie."

"They might be asleep."

"I do not believe so. I saw lights on inside earlier, when we were out by the shed. She might be nervous with the power outage."

"Good idea."

She knocked softly on the door. "Jen? This is Rosa. Are you all right?"

A moment later the door opened. Jen held a candle in one hand and a flashlight in the other.

Rosa couldn't see her face well, but her blue eyes seemed huge in the dim light.

"Everything is fine here," Jen said. "Thank you for checking." She suddenly noticed Wyatt and seemed to freeze. "Oh. I thought you were alone."

Rosa shook her head. "Wyatt helped me fix the banging door on the garden shed and now he seems to think I need his help or I will fall down the stairs."

"How nice of him to help you." Jen smiled a little, though her anxiety still seemed palpable. "Quite a storm, isn't it?"

"Yes. But do not worry. The power should be

back on soon. I see you have a flashlight. Do you need anything else?"

"Only for the power to come back on." Jen's gaze shifted down the stairs behind them, as if she expected someone else to come racing up any moment.

Oh, the poor thing. She had been through so very much. Rosa's heart broke all over again for her.

She knew very well what it felt like to be so afraid of what might be lurking around every dark corner. Rosa had seen plenty of real boogeymen in her life and knew that reality could be worse than any horror movie.

That was a long time ago, she reminded herself. A world away from this beautiful house, which might or might not contain a friendly spirit who smelled like flowers.

She tried to give Jen a reassuring smile. "It should not be long," she repeated. "But if you need anything at all—even company—you know where to find me. In fact, if you would like, you and Addie could sleep in my guestroom."

Jen looked up the stairs as if tempted by the idea, then shook her head. "We should be all right. It's only a storm. But thank you."

Impulsively, Rosa reached out and hugged the other woman, sensing Jen needed reassurance as much as Rosa did.

"Good night, my friend. Everything will be better in the morning. That is what my mother always told me."

"I might have to hold you to that."

Jen waved at them both then closed the door. Rosa could hear the sound of the dead bolt locking. Good. Jen could not be too careful.

She and Wyatt continued up the final flight of stairs. She had not locked her door when she'd left in such a hurry. Behind it, she could hear Fiona whining.

She hurried to open it and was met with a warm, worried dog, who came bounding out to lick her hand.

"I'm here. Safe and sound, darling. Were you worried about me? I am so sorry I left you."

She rubbed her dog until Fi settled down enough to go over to investigate Wyatt.

He reached an absent hand down to pet her. Here on her apartment landing in the dim light of the flashlight, a quiet intimacy seemed to swirl between them.

She wanted to kiss him.

The urge came over her, fiercely undeniable.

She *had* to deny it. She should get that crazy thought out of her head immediately. Wyatt wasn't the man for her and he never would be.

It was hard to remember that now, here in this

cozy nook with the rain pounding against the glass and his scent swirling around her.

"What is your neighbor downstairs running from?"

Rosa tensed, all thought of kissing him gone in her instant defensiveness over Jen.

"What makes you say that?"

"I've been in law enforcement for a long time. I can tell when someone is scared of something. Jen is frightened, isn't she?"

She could not betray her friend's confidence. If Jen wanted Wyatt to know what had happened to her over the past year, she would have to be the one to tell him.

"I cannot tell you this."

"Can't? Or won't?"

"What is the difference? She is my friend. Her business is her business."

"Just like your secrets are your own?"

What did he know about her secrets? Rosa felt panic flare. Carrie would not have told him what she knew, would she?

No. She could not believe that. Carrie had agreed never to tell anyone the things she knew about Rosa's past and she trusted her friend completely.

"Everyone has secrets, do they not? Some they share with those they trust, some they prefer to keep to themselves."

He was quiet for a long moment. "I hope you know that if you ever want to share yours, you can trust me."

She trusted very few people. And she certainly wasn't going to trust Wyatt, who was only a temporary tenant.

"If I had any secrets, I might do that. But I don't. I'm a completely open book."

She tried for a breezy smile but could tell he wasn't at all convinced. In fact, he looked slightly disappointed.

She tried to ignore her guilt and opted to change the subject instead. "The lightning seems to have stopped for now. I am sure the power will be back on soon."

"No doubt."

"Thank you again for coming to my rescue. Good night. Be careful going back down the stairs."

"I will do that. Good night."

He studied her, his features unreadable in the dim light of her flashlight. He looked as if he wanted to say something else. Instead, he shook his head slightly.

"Good night."

As he turned to go back down the stairs, the masculine scent of him swirled toward her. She felt that sudden wild urge to kiss him again but ignored it. Instead, she went into her darkened apartment, her dog at her heels, and firmly closed the door behind her, wishing she could close the door to her thoughts as easily.

Chapter Four

He didn't want this.

As Wyatt returned down the stairs at Brambleberry House, his own flashlight illuminating the way ahead of him, his thoughts were tangled and dark.

He didn't want to be attracted to Rosa but couldn't seem to shake her image. The high cheekbones, the warm, dark eyes, the mouth that looked soft and delicious.

He had wanted to taste that mouth, with a hunger he hadn't known for a long time.

He didn't want it. He wasn't ready. He didn't know if he ever would be.

Tori had been the love of his life. His childhood sweetheart. He had loved her fiercely and wholeheartedly.

She had been funny and smart, a little acerbic sometimes but kind. A dedicated school guidance counselor, she had loved her students, their home, their family.

He had fully expected they would have a lifetime together. Her death, especially coming out of nowhere, had shattered Wyatt's entire world. For the last three years, he had done his best to glue back together the pieces, for Logan's sake.

He thought he had done a pretty good job for his son. He knew Logan missed his mother. How could he not? Tori left a huge hole to fill. But by moving to Cannon Beach, Wyatt had made sure Logan had his aunt Carrie to fill in some of those gaps. She was there with hugs at the end of the school day, she baked him cookies and she helped him with his homework.

His son was happy. That was the most important thing.

As for Wyatt, he knew he couldn't stay in this odd limbo forever.

For the first two years, he had been in a daze just trying to survive with work and being a single father. About six months ago, he had started dating a little here and there, mostly going out to lunch or coffee while Logan was in school.

Those experiences had been such a bust that he had decided he wasn't ready to move on.

Maybe he would never be ready.

He would be okay with that, though he knew Tori wouldn't have wanted him to be alone forever.

He kept recalling a conversation between them when they were driving home from some event or other, just a month before her death. Almost as if she'd had some instinctive premonition, Tori had brought up what should happen if one of them died.

He worked in law enforcement, was at much higher risk for a premature death, so he had assumed she had been thinking about what she would do if *he* died.

They both said they wanted the other one to move on and find happiness again. She had been insistent about it, actually, saying she would hate thinking about him being lonely and would haunt him forever if he didn't find another woman.

Maybe she and Abigail were in cahoots. The thought made him smile a little, imagining a couple of ghostly matchmakers, scheming in the background.

Now that the raw pain of losing Tori had faded to a quiet, steady ache, Wyatt knew he should probably start thinking about the rest of his life.

He wasn't ready, though. The past three years had been so hard, he didn't know if he could ever

risk his heart again—and there was no point in
even thinking about it in connection to someone
like Rosa Galvez, who didn't seem to like him
very much.

Rosa had secrets. He had known that for some
time. She always seemed evasive and tense whenever he was around, especially on the rare occa-
sions he was wearing his badge.

Maybe she didn't like the police. He knew there
were plenty of people in that camp, for some very
justifiable reasons.

She could keep her secrets. They were none of
his business. He was living in her house for only a
short time and then he and Logan would be back in
their own home, away from a woman who smelled
like vanilla and berries and made him ache for
things he wasn't ready to want again.

A major fraud investigation kept him busy over
the next week and Wyatt didn't see much of his
lovely landlady or his intriguing, skittish neighbor on the second floor. He was grateful, he told
himself. At least about the former. He didn't need
any more temptation in the form of Rosa Galvez.

He had decided it was easier all around to pretend his attraction to her was only a figment of
his imagination.

By the Friday of the week after the storm,
Fourth of July weekend, he was looking forward

to extended time with Logan. He had the weekend off and he and his son had a whole list of fun
things to do before he had to go back to work on
Monday—fishing, going for a bike ride and picking out new furniture for Logan's room in their
house.

Right now, his focus was dinner. Wyatt hadn't
given any thought to what to fix and Hank was
running around in circles after spending all day
cooped up.

He decided to solve both problems at the same
time. "Why don't we take him for a walk down the
beach and grab some dinner at the taco truck?"

"Tacos!" Logan exclaimed joyfully, setting
down the controller of his device.

After Wyatt changed out of his shirt and tie and
into casual weekend attire, they hooked up Hank's
leash—a tricky undertaking while the dog jumped
around with excitement.

Neither Rosa nor Jen and her daughter were
out in the large yard of Brambleberry House as he
and Logan walked through the garden toward the
beach gate at the back of the property.

The early evening was beautiful, the air scented
with the flowers blooming all around them.

Though it was still a few hours from sunset, the
sun had begun to slide toward the water, coloring
the clouds orange as it went.

The beach was crowded with weekend visitors.

Everybody seemed in a good mood, which was one of the benefits of working in a town frequented by tourists.

"What did you do at camp today?" he asked Logan as they walked across the sand. With Carrie's help, Wyatt had been lucky enough to find a place for his son in one of the most popular science day camps in town.

"Tons of stuff. We went tide pooling and I saw about a zillion starfish and a cool purple anemone. And when we had free time, I played on the slide with my friend Carlos, mostly."

"Do I know Carlos?"

"He just moved here and he's my age. He likes *Star Wars*, just like me."

Logan went on to enumerate the many wonderful qualities of his new friend as they walked a few blocks along the packed sand toward the parking lot just above the beach, where their favorite taco truck usually parked.

"And after lunch and free time, we did another art project, the one I showed you. And then you came to get me to go home."

"Sounds like a fun-packed day."

"Yeah," Logan said cheerfully just as they turned up toward the taco truck.

"There it is. Yay. I'm starving!"

Seven-year-old boys always seemed to be starving. "Are you going to get the usual? A soft chicken taco and a churro?"

"Yes!"

The taco truck was busy, as usual. The food here was fresh and invariably delicious. He and Logan joined the queue and were talking about some of the things they planned to do that weekend when Logan's face suddenly brightened.

"Look who's here! Hi, Rosa. Hi, Fiona. Hank, look. It's your friend Fiona!"

Hank sidled up to greet Fiona with enthusiastic sniffing, as if they hadn't seen each other for months, while Wyatt tried to calm the ridiculous acceleration of his heartbeat.

He had not been able to stop thinking about Rosa since the night of the storm.

She beamed at his son but avoided meeting his gaze. Was it deliberate or accidental?

"*¡Buenas,* Logan! *¿Cómo estás?*"

"I don't know what that means."

"It means 'good evening. How are you?'"

"How do I say I'm good?"

"You can say *soy bueno* or just *bueno.*"

"*Bueno,*" Logan said, parroting her. "*¿Cómo estás?*"

She smiled. "*Soy buena.*"

Wyatt had to again fight the urge to kiss her, right there in front of everyone in line.

"This is our favorite taco truck," Logan told her.

"Do you like tacos, too? Oh, yeah. You probably do because you speak Spanish."

He winced at his son's cultural misassumption but Rosa didn't seem offended. "Except I am from a country called Honduras and these are tacos from Mexico. I like them very much, though. The owner is also my friend."

They reached the order window at that moment and the owner in question, Jose Herrera, ignored Wyatt for a moment to greet Rosa in Spanish.

Wyatt had taken high-school Spanish and had tried to work on his language skills over the years. Unfortunately, he still understood best when Spanish speakers spoke slowly, which didn't happen often in general conversation.

He had no idea what the guy said. Whatever it was, it made Rosa laugh. She answered him in rapid-fire Spanish, which sparked a belly laugh in Herrera.

"Go ahead and order," Wyatt said to her.

"You were here first."

"We're still trying to decide," he lied.

She gave her order then stepped aside for him and Logan to do the same.

"Don't forget my churro," Logan instructed.

"How could I?" Wyatt smiled at his son.

When he finished, the three of them moved together to one of the open picnic tables set around the truck that overlooked the beach.

"And how are you, Señor Logan?" Rosa asked.

"Señor means 'mister.' We learned that in school."

"You are correct."

"I am fine. I like living in your house. It's friendly."

She smiled with warm delight. "I am so happy you think so. Some houses, they are cold. Brambleberry House is not that way. When you step inside, you feel like you are home."

"And it always smells good, too. Like flowers," Logan said.

Rosa met Wyatt's gaze with an expressive eyebrow, as if to say *See? I told you.*

"Aren't we lucky to live in such a nice place with beautiful flower gardens that smell so good?" Wyatt replied blandly.

"How is your house coming along?"

Was she in a hurry to get rid of them? No. Rosa had been nothing but accommodating.

"We're making progress. They're painting soon, then we need to do the finish carpentry."

"That *is* progress. You will be home before you know it, back in your own bedroom. Your dog will like that, yes?"

He loved listening to her talk, completely entranced by her slight accent and unique phrasing. Okay, the truth was, he was completely entranced by *her*. She could read a lawn-mower instruction manual and he would find her fascinating.

"I think so far he's having fun being friends with Fiona," Logan said.

The two dogs did seem pretty enamored of each other. Hank hadn't been around a lot of other dogs and it was good to see him getting along well with the Irish setter.

Rosa smiled at his son. "Fiona can be a charmer. She is quite hard to resist."

That made two of them. Wyatt sighed. This had to stop. He didn't want this attraction. Even after a short time, he still hadn't come to terms with his growing interest in his landlady.

Seeing her again here in the July sunshine, bright and vibrant and lovely, only intensified the ache that had been growing since the night of the storm.

He pursed his lips, determined not to think about that. "How is Jen settling in, living in Cannon Beach?"

He had only seen the second-floor tenant in passing a few times. She still seemed as anxious and uncomfortable around him as before.

"Good, as far as I know. She and Addie seem content for now."

Something told him that was a new state of affairs. He didn't know what the woman was going through but was glad at least that she was finding peace here.

"We bumped into Addie and Jen at the grocery store the other night. Jen seems a little uncomfortable around me."

If he hoped Rosa might take the bait and tell him what was going on with Jen, he was doomed to disappointment. She quickly changed the subject away from her friend.

"I'm sure I don't know why. Logan, did I see you walking past my store window today with a bucket?"

"I don't know. Maybe. My day camp went tide-pooling."

"Oh, I love doing that at low tide. What did you see?"

"About a zillion sea stars and some anemone and a sea cucumber. Only it's not the kind you can eat."

"How wonderful. Is it not fun to see what can be found beneath the water?"

"Yeah. It's like another whole world," Logan said. He started regaling Rosa with a few stories of interesting things he had seen during previous tide-pooling trips.

"My teacher said you can sometimes go snorkeling and be right in the water looking at some different habitats. That would be fun, don't you think?"

"Yes. Very fun. Maybe your father should take you to Hawaii. Or to my country, Honduras."

Logan's face lit up. "Can we go, Dad? And can Rosa come with us?"

Wyatt cleared his throat, his mind suddenly full of images of warm tropical nights and soft, flower-scented breezes.

"That would be fun. But Rosa has a busy job here. She probably wouldn't have time."

Logan seemed unconcerned. "Maybe we could go with Aunt Carrie, Uncle Joe and Bella. That would be fun, too."

Not as fun as Hawaii or Honduras with Rosa, but, of course, Wyatt couldn't say that. To his re-lief, a moment later Logan's attention was diverted from snorkeling and travel when he saw another friend from school ride up to the taco truck along with her parents on bikes.

"There's my friend Sadie," he announced. "I need to tell her something."

He handed the leash to Wyatt and hurried over to talk to his friend. Wyatt realized that left him alone at the table to make conversation with Rosa.

"What part of Honduras are you from?"

He didn't miss the way she tensed a little, then seemed to force herself to relax. "A small fishing village near the coast. I left when I was a teenager."

"How did you go from a small village in Honduras to living at Brambleberry House and running a gift shop on the Oregon coast?"

She shrugged. "A long story. The short version is that *mi Tia* Anna is part owner of the house, along with her friend Sage. Anna and her husband live in Portland while Sage and her family spend most of their time in California. Anna needed someone to run the gift shop for her. I have a retail marketing degree and was working a job I didn't enjoy that much in Park City."

"Utah?"

"Yes. Have you been there?"

"No. I'm not much of a skier. My parents used to take us to Mount Hood when I was a kid. I never really enjoyed it."

She smiled a little. "I do not ski, either. It seems a silly pastime to me."

"I guess some people like the thrill. You're not an adrenaline junkie?"

"No. Not me. I have had enough adventure for a lifetime, thank you."

He wanted to pursue that line of questioning but didn't have a chance as Logan and their food arrived at the picnic table at the same time.

They had never really made a conscious decision to eat together, but it somehow felt natural, especially as their dogs were nestled together and had become fast friends.

What happened to Hank's restlessness? Wyatt

wondered. Right now, the dog did not look like he wanted to move.

The food was as good as always, the chicken flavorful and the salsa spicy.

He spent a moment helping Logan get situated, then turned his attention back to Rosa. "So you were saying you lived in Utah but you don't like to ski. And that you have had enough adventure and aren't an adrenaline junkie."

She took a drink of the *horchata* she had ordered. "Utah is beautiful year-round. In the summertime, I do like to hike in the mountains and mountain-bike with my parents and *primos*. Cousins," she explained at Logan's quizzical look."

"I have one *primo*. Cousin. Her name is Bella."

Rosa smiled at him. "I know your cousin very well."

"You sound like you are close to your family," Wyatt said.

"Oh, yes. Very. My family is wonderful. My parents, Daniel and Lauren Galvez, are the most kind people you will ever meet. Daniel is in law enforcement, as well. He is the sheriff of our county."

"Is that right?" He found the information rather disheartening. If she had law-enforcement members in her own family, his occupation wasn't likely to be the reason she was so distrustful of Wyatt.

"Yes. Everyone loves him in Moose Springs and the towns nearby. And my mother, she is the doctor in town."

"The only one?"

"It is not a very big town. Some people go to Park City when they need specialists, but Lauren is the best doctor in the whole world."

She spoke of her parents by their first names, which made him wonder at the relationship.

"Is she also from Honduras?"

He wasn't surprised when her jaw tensed at the question. "No. She is from Moose Springs. Daniel, as well. They adopted me when I came to this country."

He wanted to pursue that line of questioning but reminded himself this was a casual encounter over tacos, not an interrogation. She had the right to her privacy. This was obviously a touchy subject for her and he didn't want to make her uncomfortable.

"So. What do you think of your taco?" she asked Logan.

"Muy delicioso," he said with a grin. "That means 'very delicious.' I learned that from my friend Carlos. That's what he says every day at lunch."

"That is the perfect thing to say about the tacos here. They are definitely *muy delicioso.*"

She and Logan spent a few more minutes comparing ways to gush about their meals, leaving

Wyatt to wonder what made Rosa so uncomfortable when she talked about her past.

What was she hiding? She did not like to talk about herself, which he found unusual. In his line of work, he had learned that most law-abiding people loved talking about themselves and their lives. With a few well-aimed questions, Wyatt usually could find out anything he wanted to know.

People who had things to hide, however, learned techniques to evade those kinds of questions.

Her secrets were not his business, he reminded himself. She was a private person and there was certainly no law against that.

He would be smart to remember that her history was her own. He wasn't entitled to know, especially when their only relationship was that of landlady and tenant.

Chapter Five

The man was entirely too curious.

It didn't help that she couldn't seem to keep her usual defensive techniques in place when he looked at her out of those blue eyes. She forgot about protecting herself, about concealing the parts of her life she preferred to forget. She forgot everything, lost in the totally ridiculous urge to lean across the picnic table and press her mouth against his. Anything to stop his questions.

Wouldn't that go over well? She could just imagine how he would react. It almost made her wish she had the nerve to try it.

To her relief, he seemed to give up his interrogation as they finished dinner. He sat back and let her and Logan chatter about Logan's friends, his day camp and the very cool dinosaur bones he saw at a museum in Portland with his aunt Carrie.

He was really an adorable boy, filled with life and energy. He loved *Star Wars*, Legos, his dog and his father, not necessarily in that order.

She enjoyed their company immensely, especially once Wyatt stopped digging into her life.

"Good choice on dinner, kiddo," he said with a warm smile to his son.

Seeing him with Logan was like glimpsing a different person. He was more lighthearted, and certainly more approachable. He had smiled more during dinner than she had seen in all the time she had known him.

The Townsend men were both extremely hard to resist.

"That was so yummy," Logan said as he balled up the wrapper of his taco and returned it to the tray. "Thanks, Dad."

"I didn't do much except pay for it, but you're welcome. You should tell Jose how much you enjoyed it."

At that moment, the taco-truck owner was delivering another tray to a nearby table so Logan jumped up and hurried over to him.

"*Gracias* for the taco. It was *muy delicioso.*"

Jose, bald head gleaming in the fading sunlight,

beamed down at the boy with delight. "You are welcome. You come back anytime."

He fist-bumped Logan, who skipped as he hurried back to their table.

"That was very nice of you," Rosa said. "People like to feel appreciated."

"My dad taught me we should always tell people thank you for things they do. Sometimes we might be the only ones all day who say it to them."

Rosa had to smile at that. Her gaze met Wyatt's and she found him watching her out of those unreadable blue eyes again.

"That is probably true. Then I must say thank you for sharing dinner with me. I enjoyed it very much."

"So did I," Logan said.

"As did I," Wyatt said to her surprise.

He rose and took her trash and his to the garbage can and dumped it, then returned to the table. "Are you walking back to Brambleberry House?"

"Yes."

"We're headed that way, too. We can walk together, if you want."

Did she? A smart woman would tell him she only just remembered an errand she needed to run at one of the little shops close to the taco truck. Spending more time with Wyatt and Logan was definitely dangerous to her peace of mind.

She couldn't think of anything she needed at

any of the touristy places in this area of town, anyway.

"Sure. It makes sense as we are going the same place."

Fiona jumped up from her spot beside Hank, almost as if she had been following the conversation and knew it was time to go.

Sometimes Rosa thought the dog had to be the smartest animal in the world.

As if on cue, Hank jumped up as well, then sat on his haunches and looked pointedly at his owner, as if to tell him he was ready to leave, too.

"I'll take Hank," Logan said and picked up the leash. He led the way, still chattering, as they headed along the sand toward Brambleberry House.

"Looks like it's going to be another gorgeous sunset." Wyatt looked out across the water at the clouds fanning out across the sky in shades of apricot and plum.

"Lovely."

It was the sort of beautiful, vibrant summer evening meant to be spent with a special someone.

Too bad she didn't have a special someone.

Rosa sighed. She hadn't dated anyone seriously since she moved to Cannon Beach four years earlier.

She really should go out on a date or two. All of her friends were constantly trying to set her up, but lately it all seemed like so much bother. Maybe that would distract her from this unwanted and inconvenient attraction to Wyatt.

Rosa was not a nun or anything. She dated, when she found someone worthy of her time, though it was rather depressing to realize she hadn't dated anyone seriously in a long time. Not since college, really?

For two years, she had been very close to a fellow business major whose parents had emigrated from Peru. She and Santos had talked about returning to South America to open a string of restaurants.

As far as she knew, he might have even done that. They had lost track of each other after graduation and she rarely thought of him anymore.

Santos and the few other serious relationships she'd had had taught her that sex could be beautiful and meaningful with someone she cared about.

She was happy with her life. She was running a successful business, she lived in a beautiful home and she loved the surroundings in Cannon Beach. She had good friends here and back in Utah and loved her volunteer work for the local women's shelter.

Okay, maybe she was sometimes lonely at night. Maybe she sometimes wished she could have someone to cuddle with, to talk to at the end of the day, to share her hopes and dreams.

Fiona was lovely but talking to her had its limitations since she couldn't respond.

At the same time, she was not sure she was ready for the inherent risks of trusting her heart to someone.

She had told no one else about the things that had happened to her. Not even Santos or the few other men she had dated seriously had known the entire truth. She had told them bits and pieces, but not everything.

Maybe that was why those relationships had withered and died without progressing to the next level, because she had never completely trusted them to know.

She certainly wasn't about to spill her life story to Wyatt, as much as she enjoyed the company of him and his son.

The walk back to the house passed quickly, mostly because Logan dominated the conversation. He pointed out a kite he liked, told her about riding a bike along the hard-packed sand near the water, went into a long story about the time he and his dad took a charter out to see whales up near Astoria.

"Sorry about Logan," Wyatt said in a low voice when the boy was distracted by something he saw on the sand and ran ahead with Hank to investigate. "He's in a chatty mood tonight. Some days I wish I could find a pause button for a minute."

She smiled. "I do not mind. I love listening to him. Your son is terrific."

"Agreed," he said gruffly. "He's the best seven-year-old I know, even if he does tend to show off a little in front of pretty women."

Rosa felt flustered and didn't know how to answer that. Fortunately, they had reached the beach gate at Brambleberry House.

She punched in the code and the door swung open. As they walked through the back garden, she suddenly saw a strange car in the driveway, a small late-model bright red SUV she didn't recognize.

Rosa tensed, worrying instantly for Jen. She was reaching for her phone to check in with the woman when two females hurried around the side of the house. She recognized them instantly—Carrie and Bella—and shoved her phone back into her pocket.

She smiled and waved, happy at the unexpected visit even as she could feel the usual mix of joy and tension settle over her.

"Hi!" Bella called out to all of them, waving vigorously.

"Hi, Bella," Logan shouted, then beamed toward Rosa. "That's my cousin, Bella, and her mom."

"It is good to see them," Rosa said.

As they moved toward each other, she thought she saw Carrie look between her and Wyatt with a surprised sort of look, as if she wouldn't have expected to see them walking up from the beach together.

"There you are! We rang both your doorbells but nobody answered."

"We bumped into each other while we were grabbing dinner and walked back together," Rosa said quickly, so that his sister didn't get the wrong idea about the two of them.

"We got tacos at the food truck."

"Oh, I love that place," Bella gushed. "My friends and I like to stop there after school. I love their churros."

"Me, too," Logan declared, as if the cinnamon and sugar still dusting his clothes wasn't enough of a giveaway.

Rosa had to smile. She thought she saw Carrie give her a speculative sort of look but couldn't be certain.

"I came by to show off my new wheels," her friend said. "What do you think?"

"Let's take a look," Wyatt said.

They moved toward the driveway and the small red SUV.

"Nice," Wyatt said, walking around the vehicle to check it out.

"I like your new car," Logan said. "It's pretty."

"Thank you, dear." Carrie beamed at him.

"And guess what?" Bella's voice vibrated with

excitement. "We're keeping Mom's old car and when I start learning how to drive, I get to practice in that one."

Driving. Bella would be driving in only a few more years. How was it possible that she had grown so much?

"There's plenty of time for that," Wyatt said, looking alarmed.

"Not really. In less than two years, I'll be old enough to get my learner's permit. I'll be driving around town before you know it."

"Good luck with that," Wyatt said to his sister.

"I know. I remember Dad teaching me how to drive. It was a nightmare. And I believe you wrecked a car or two in your day."

"You wrecked cars, Uncle Wyatt?" Bella looked at him wide-eyed and so did his son.

Wyatt gave his sister a rueful look. "One. And it wasn't my fault. A guy T-boned me in an intersection. He got the citation."

"In that case, I'm sorry I impugned your driving credentials," Carrie said.

He shrugged. "I will confess that in the past, I might have had a propensity to drive too fast. Good thing I can do that legally now, with lights and sirens going."

He tapped Bella lightly on the head. "But remember, I'm a highly trained officer of the law.

You should always stay within the legal speed limit."

Bella giggled. "What about you, Rosa. Where did you learn to drive? Here or in Honduras?"

She always felt strange talking about her childhood life with Bella and Carrie. "Here. My father taught me when I was in high school. He and my mother were tired of driving me to after-school activities all the time. We had many ranch roads in Utah, where they live, so we practiced for hours until I could feel comfortable behind the wheel."

That was one more gift Lauren and Daniel had given her. Independence. They had wanted her to have all the skills she would need to make a success of her life. She knew they were proud of what she had done and how far she had come. At the same time, she knew Lauren especially worried about her love life.

What would Lauren think about Wyatt? Rosa could guess. She would probably adore him—first because he was in law enforcement like Daniel and second because he was a good man who loved his child.

She would be over the moon if she had any idea how Rosa couldn't seem to stop thinking about him.

She didn't plan to tell either of them about her new tenant. Her parents and siblings were coming to town just before Labor Day, but Logan and

Wyatt would be back in their own home by then. She would have to tell them nothing.

Oddly, the thought of the Townsends moving out left her feeling slightly depressed.

"When I get my learner's permit," Bella said, "I'm going to need a lot of practice time. Rosa, maybe you and Uncle Wyatt can help and give my mom and dad a break so they don't always have to ride with me."

Rosa couldn't find words for a few seconds, she was so honored that Bella would even consider allowing her to help her learn how to drive.

"I would enjoy that," she said, her voice a little ragged.

"It's a deal," Wyatt said. "It will be good practice for when I have to teach this kiddo how to drive."

Would she be here when Bella was learning how to drive? Rosa wasn't sure. She had never intended to stay in Cannon Beach for long, but once she had moved here, it had been hard to drag herself away. Now that she was a part owner of the gift store, it became even more difficult.

She didn't like thinking about leaving all the friends she had made here, but perhaps she would one day find it inevitable.

"Showing off my car wasn't the only reason we dropped by. I know you have the weekend off. Joe and I were thinking of grilling steaks and then watching the fireworks on Sunday. We would love to have you. Rosa, you're invited as well. And your friend Jen, if she would like to come."

Rosa wasn't sure if she was ready to have another social outing with the irresistible Townsend men. On the other hand, how could she refuse an invitation from Carrie?

At her hesitation, Carrie made a face. "I know it's rude to just drop in with an invitation two days beforehand. I should have planned better. Please don't worry if you already have plans. But if you can come, we will eat at about seven thirty."

"I do not have plans," she said. In truth, she had been so busy at work, she had not given the holiday weekend much thought.

She could handle a few hours in Wyatt's company. She would simply spend the evening talking with Carrie and Bella.

"Dinner would be nice. What should I bring?"

"Yourself. That's the main thing. But if you want to bring a salad or a fruit plate, that's always good."

She nodded. "Yes. I can do that."

"Oh, lovely. We will see you Sunday, then. Now we're off to take this beauty for a drive down the coast. With me behind the wheel, of course," she assured them, which made Bella moan in mock disappointment.

A moment later, she stood beside Wyatt and watched the little red SUV back out of the driveway.

"Your sister. She is wonderful."

Rosa could not even put into words her deep gratitude toward Carrie.

"She is pretty terrific. Our mom had breast cancer when I was in high school and Carrie basically stepped in to take care of all of us while Mom was having treatment. She was a young bride herself but that didn't stop her."

"That is wonderful. My mother died of breast cancer when I was fourteen."

She wasn't sure why she told him that. It was another part of her past she didn't usually share.

He gave her a sympathetic look. "I'm sorry. That's a hard loss for a teenager."

She had been so frightened after her mother died. She had no one to share her pain except a few of her mother's friends.

They had been as poor as Rosa and her mother and couldn't help her survive when they were barely subsisting. She had known she was on her own from the moment her mother had died.

That cold truth had led her to making some terrible decisions, with consequences she could never have imagined.

"Hey, Dad, can I show Rosa what I built out of Legos this week?"

Wyatt shook his head. "We've taken up her whole evening. I'm sure she has things to do."

Rosa did have things to do, always. Most small-business owners never really stopped working, even if it was only the constantly turning wheels of their subconscious.

But at the disappointed look on Logan's face, she smiled at the boy. "I do have things to do tonight but I would love to see your creation first."

She could tell Wyatt wasn't particularly pleased at her answer. Why not? Was he in a hurry to get rid of her? Too bad. He could survive a few more moments of her company, for his son's sake.

Wyatt unlocked the front door. As she stood in the entryway waiting for him to open his apartment, Rosa smelled the distinctive scent of flowers that had no logical reason to be there.

Hank sniffed the air and so did Fiona. They both went to the bottom of the stairs, wagging their tails.

Apparently, Abigail was active tonight. Rosa rolled her eyes at her own imagination. She did not believe in ghosts, benevolent or otherwise. If she did, she would never be able to sleep for all the ghosts haunting her.

The dogs followed them as they went into the ground-floor apartment.

"My room is back here," Logan said. He grabbed

Rosa's hand and tugged her in the direction of his space.

A *Star Wars* blanket covered the bed and toys were scattered around the room. It made her happy to see the signs a child lived there, and somehow she had the feeling it would have made Abigail happy, too.

"It's over here. This was the biggest set I've ever made. It had over two hundred pieces! I wasn't sure I could do it but my dad helped me."

He showed her a complicated-looking brick masterpiece, which she recognized as a space-craft from one of the *Star Wars* movies, though she couldn't have said for sure which one.

It warmed her heart to think about the boy and his father working together on the project.

"How wonderful. It must have taken you a long time."

"Not really. It's not that hard if you follow the picture directions. My friend Carlos got one, too, and he was able to put it together and Carlos can't even read in English very much."

"Can't he?"

"He's getting better." Logan looked as if he didn't want to disrespect his friend. "Anyway, he hasn't been here very long, only a few months. He told me he speaks Spanish at home all the time. I want to learn Spanish so I can talk to him better but I don't know very many words."

His eyes suddenly grew wide. "Hey. You speak Spanish *and* English. You could teach me."

"Me?" Rosa was so shocked at the suggestion that she didn't quite know how to respond.

"Rosa is very busy with her store," Wyatt said from the doorway. "We don't need to bother her. You and I can keep reading the books and practicing with the language app on my phone."

How could she be anything but charmed at the idea of Wyatt and his son trying to learn Spanish together so Logan could talk to his friend?

"I would not mind practicing with you when I can," she said quickly. "I should tell you that I have been speaking mostly English almost as long as I spoke only Spanish, so some of my vocabulary might be a little rusty."

"Oh, yay! Thanks, Rosa. *Gracias.*"

"*De nada.* I am usually home after six most nights. You can come knock on my door and if I'm home, we can practice a little in the evening."

"Cool! Thanks!"

To her shock, her gave her a quick, impulsive hug. Her arms went around him and she closed her eyes for a moment, grateful for this tender mercy.

When she opened her eyes, she found Wyatt watching her with a strange look in his eyes.

"Okay. Bath time. Tell Rosa good-night, then go find your pajamas and underwear. The clean ones are still in the dryer."

"How do I say 'good night' again?"

"*Buenas noches*. Or sometimes just *buenas*."

He repeated the words, then hurried off to find his pajamas.

"Thanks for your patience with us," Wyatt said in a low voice after the boy had left.

"I do not mind. He is a sweet boy. I enjoy his company."

And yours, she wanted to add. *Even when I know I should not.*

"If you don't really have time to practice Spanish with him, don't worry about it. He'll probably forget by tomorrow morning."

She frowned. "I will not forget. I promised to help him and I would not make a promise I did not intend to keep."

He looked down at her, that odd light in his eyes again. "An admirable quality in a person."

She was not admirable. At all. If he knew her better, he would know that.

"I meant what I said. I will be happy to help him. Send him up any evening he is free or even outside when I am working in the yard. I do not know if I would be a good teacher, but I will do my best."

"I'm sure you will be great," he said. "I just don't want my son to bother you."

"He is never a bother. I will enjoy it."

"Thank you, then. He will probably learn faster

from a native speaker than any app could teach him."

"I will do my best," she said again. "Now if you will excuse me, I must go."

She really needed to leave soon, before she did something foolish like throw herself into his arms.

"Good night," she said, edging toward the door.

"Buenas noches," he replied, with a credible pronunciation. "I guess I'll see you on Sunday at Carrie's house."

Oh. Right. She had almost forgotten the invitation. "Yes. I guess so."

"We could always walk over together."

What would Carrie think if the two of them came together to her dinner party? Rosa suspected his sister was already getting the wrong idea about them after seeing them together tonight.

Still, it made sense. It would be silly to drive when the house was so close. "All right. Come, Fiona," she called.

Her dog rose from the rug, where she was cuddled with Hank, and gave the little dog a sorrowful look, then followed Rosa up the stairs to her apartment.

Something seemed to have shifted between her and Wyatt during this evening spent together, but she couldn't have said exactly what.

He was attracted to her.

She wasn't sure how she knew that but she did.

Maybe that look in his eyes as he had watched his son hug her... Touched, surprised...hungry.

She was imagining things. Wyatt Townsend was certainly not hungry for her.

If he was, it was only because he didn't know the truth. All the secrets of her past, which she had pushed into the deep corners of herself, where no one else could see.

Chapter Six

Summer evenings along the Oregon coast could be magical, especially when they were clear, with no sign of coastal fog.

As they walked the short distance between Brambleberry House and his sister's place on Sunday, the air smelled of the sea, mingled with pine and cedar and the flowers that seemed to grow in abundance this time of year, spilling out of flower baskets and brightening gardens.

Independence Day turned out to be perfect. He and Logan had spent the morning fishing in their favorite spot along the nearby river. Even though the fishing was a bust and they didn't catch anything big enough to keep, Logan still had a great time.

Afterward, they had gone on a hike at one of their favorite trails in Ecola State Park and then had spent the afternoon playing in the sand.

He wouldn't be surprised if Logan fell asleep early.

Of course, he wasn't anywhere close to sleeping now. He was having too much fun quizzing Rosa about the Spanish word for everything they passed.

"How do you say *mailbox*?" Logan asked, pointing to a row of them across the road.

"Buzón."

"And *house* is *casa*, right?"

"Yes. Very good. And we are walking. *Estamos caminando*."

"Yes. To my aunt Carrie's *casa*."

She smiled down at him, looking bright and lovely in the golden evening light. To himself, Wyatt could admit that the main reason the evening seemed particularly beautiful had to do with the woman he was walking beside.

"Excellent," she said. "You and Carlos will be jabbering up a storm in Spanish before you know it."

"I think his English will always be better than my Spanish."

"But you are trying to learn for your friend. That is the important thing. It was very hard for me when I came to this country and could not always find the words I wanted. I am grateful I had very patient family and friends to help me."

He had to wonder again at her story. She had said her mother died when she was fourteen, which meant she had probably come here by herself. But what were the circumstances that had led to her being adopted by a family in Utah?

None of his business, he reminded himself. She was his landlady, nothing more, though it was hard to remember that on an evening like this, especially when his son slipped his hand in hers, as if it was the most natural thing in the world.

Rosa looked down at Logan and their joined hands with an expression of astonishment, and then one of wonder, that touched Wyatt deeply.

"How do you say *whale*?" Logan asked when they passed a house that had a little whale-shaped bench out front.

"Ballena."

"What about *tree*?"

"Arborio."

"How about *library*?"

"Biblioteca."

Rosa never seemed to lose her patience with the constant barrage of questions. He could only guess how relieved she must have been when they reached Carrie and Joe's house a short time later.

"Now you tell me. What was *door* again?" she asked him as they approached the porch.

"*Puerta.*"

"No. *Puerto. Puerta* means *port.*"

"It's so confusing!"

"English is far more confusing," she said with a laugh. "Try figuring out the difference between *there*, *they're* and *their.*"

"I guess."

"You are doing great. We will keep practicing."

His son was already enamored with Rosa. They had practiced together the night before while Rosa was working in the small vegetable garden at the house. Wyatt had come out ahead in the arrangement, as she had sent Logan back to their apartment with a bowl of fresh green beans and another of raspberries, his favorite.

He always felt a little weird just walking into his sister's house, even though he had been living there only a few weeks earlier. He usually preferred to ring the doorbell, but this time he didn't have to. Bella opened the door before they could and grinned at them. "I saw you all walking up. *Hola.*"

"*Hola.*" Rosa's features softened. "That's a very cute shirt. Is it new?"

Bella twirled around to show off her patriotic red, white and blue polka-dotted T-shirt. "Yeah. I picked it up this afternoon on clearance. It was super cheap."

"I like it very much," Rosa said.

"I'm going with some friends to watch the fireworks in Manzanita."

He thought he saw disappointment flash in Rosa's dark eyes before she quickly concealed it. "Oh. That will be fun for you."

"I'm going to go play on the swings," Logan announced, then headed out to the elaborate play area in the backyard.

"I'll take these into the kitchen," Wyatt said, lifting the woven bag that contained the bowl of Rosa's salad, the one he had insisted on taking from her when they met up outside Brambleberry House for the walk here.

He found his sister in the kitchen slicing tomatoes. He kissed her cheek and she smiled. "You're here. Oh, and Rosa's here, too. You came together."

"Yes," Rosa said. "It was such a beautiful evening for a walk. I made a fruit salad with strawberries from my garden."

"Oh, yum. How is your garden this year? I've had so much trouble with my flowers. I think I have some kind of bug."

"They are good," Rosa replied. "Not as lovely as when Sonia was here to take care of them but I do my best with it."

"I miss Sonia," Carrie said. "I guess we should call her Elizabeth now."

Rosa nodded. "I will always think of her as Sonia, I am afraid."

Wyatt knew the story of Rosa's previous tenant. For several years, she had lived in Cannon Beach as Sonia Davis but a year earlier, she had admitted her real name was Elizabeth Hamilton. For many complicated reasons, she had been living under a different name during her time here, until her husband showed up out of the blue one day to take her back to their hometown. It had been the talk of Cannon Beach for weeks.

Rosa had been good friends with her tenant and Carrie had told him how astonished she had been at the revelation that the woman she thought she knew had so many secrets.

"How is Sonia Elizabeth?" Carrie asked, the name some of the woman's friends had taken to calling her. "Do you ever talk to her?"

"Oh, yes. We speak often," Rosa said. "I texted her the other day to ask her a question about a plant I didn't recognize and we did a video call so she could take a better look at it. She seemed happy. Her children are happy. She said she isn't having seizures much anymore and she and her husband are even talking about taking in a foster child with the idea of adopting."

Carrie looked thrilled at the news. "Oh, that's lovely. Do you know, I was thinking about Sonia the other day. I bumped into Melissa and Eli and Skye at the grocery store. Do you see them much?"

Melissa Fielding Sanderson had been another tenant of Brambleberry House. She had married a doctor, Eli Sanderson, whom Wyatt had known when he used to visit his grandmother here during his childhood.

"Oh, yes," Rosa answered. "We still meet for lunch or dinner about once a month. She's very busy with the new baby."

"Thomas is such a sweetheart," Bella said. "I watched him last week when Melissa had a test."

Melissa, a registered nurse, was studying to be a nurse practitioner and juggled school with being a mother and working at the clinic with her husband and father-in-law. Somehow she made it all work.

"What time is Jaycee's mom picking you up?" Carrie asked her daughter.

"Not until eight."

"Then you probably have time to eat with us. Why don't you and Rosa start carrying things out to the patio? We thought it would be nice to eat outside and take advantage of the gorgeous weather. Bell, you can take the plates and silverware and Rosa can take these salads."

Rosa looked delighted, which Wyatt thought was odd. Maybe she was just happy to have a task.

"Yes. That is a wonderful idea. I am happy to help."

She picked up the fruit salad she had brought and the green salad Carrie had just finished preparing, then carried them through the back door to the patio. Bella joined her, arms laden with plates and the little basket full of silverware Carrie used for outdoor entertaining. As they opened the door, Wyatt caught the delicious scent of sizzling steak.

"What can I do?"

"I think that is it for now." Carrie paused, then gave him a meaningful look. "Rosa is lovely, isn't she?"

Oh, no. He knew where this was going. Carrie seemed to think it was her job now to find him dates. She was always trying to set him up with women she knew, despite his repeated attempts to convince her he was perfectly happy and not interested in dating right now.

He gave her a stern look, though he feared it would do no good. Carrie wasn't great at taking hints.

"Yes. She's lovely."

"Inside and out," his sister said, then gave a careful look to make sure she and Bella were busy setting the patio table.

"You know, so many people could have let what she has been through turn them bitter and angry. Not Rosa. I think it's only made her stronger and more empathetic to everyone."

Wyatt frowned. "What has she been through?"

Carrie gave him a vague look. "Oh, you know. Life in general. Coming here when she was young. Losing her mother when she was just a girl."

What else did she know about Rosa's background? He wanted to push, but then had to remind himself that he was already becoming too entangled in her world. The more he learned about her, the harder it was becoming to fight off this attraction.

Bella came back into the kitchen as he was wrestling against his curiosity to know everything he could about the intriguing Rosa Galvez.

"What else can we take out?" she asked. "Also, Dad is asking for a platter for the steaks."

Carrie pulled one out of the cabinet above the refrigerator and handed it to Bella, who immediately headed back outside with it.

"I only meant to say that Rosa is a lovely woman," she said when they were alone again. "When you're ready to start thinking about dating again, she would be an excellent choice."

Wyatt shifted, vowing to do his best that evening to keep his sister from figuring out that he was already fiercely drawn to Rosa. Once she realized that, Carrie would never give up trying to push them together.

"What if I'm never ready?"

"Oh, don't say that." His sister looked anguished. "You are a young, healthy man. You can't spend the rest of your life alone, for your sake or for Logan's. You know Tori would never have wanted that."

Yes. He knew. That conversation with her had been running through his head more and more often. But a hypothetical discussion with his wife when he still thought they would have the rest of their lives together was one thing. The reality of letting someone else into his heart was something else entirely.

He was tired of being alone, though. Maybe there had been a few nights lately when he had thought it might be lovely to have someone in his life again. Someone to make him laugh, to help him not take himself so seriously, to remind him that life was a beautiful, complex mix of joy and hardship.

Even if he was ready to move on, he sensed that Rosa wasn't that person. She was wonderful with Logan but it was clear she didn't trust *him*.

Just as well. Since he *wasn't* ready, there was no point in dwelling on the issue, especially on a sweet summer night.

Rosa always loved spending time with the Abbotts. Joe and Carrie were deeply in love, even after being married more than twenty years. They held hands often, they touched all the time and they kissed at random moments.

And Bella. Being around the girl was a unique experience, like constantly walking a razor wire between joy and pain.

At dinner, Bella wanted to tell Rosa all about a boy she liked named Charlie, who might or might not be going to the same place in the nearby town to watch the fireworks.

"I really like him but I'm not allowed to date until I'm sixteen. That's not fair, is it?"

Rosa looked over to where Carrie was talking to Joe and Wyatt. She did *not* want to interject herself into a dispute between Bella and her parents over rules.

"I think that your parents have your best interests at heart. You should listen to them."

Bella clearly did not welcome that answer. "It's not like we're going to go somewhere and make out. We're watching fireworks with about a billion other people."

Rosa did not want to come across as a boring old woman but she also felt compelled to offer some advice. Bella looked on her as an older sister of sorts, just the person who *should* be giving counsel.

"You should stay with your friend and her parents, especially since they are giving you a ride."

"I know. I would never ditch my friends over a boy, no matter how cute he is."

"What cute boy are you talking about?" Carrie asked, overhearing her daughter's words.

Bella looked as if she didn't want to answer her mother but she finally sighed. "Charlie. He texted me to tell me he might be going to the fireworks."

Carrie looked vaguely alarmed. "You didn't tell me that."

"Because I knew you would blow everything out of proportion. We're not going together. I might not even see him there."

She gave Rosa an annoyed look, as if it was *her* fault Carrie had overheard their conversation.

"I don't even know if I like him that much," Bella said. "You don't have to make a big deal about it."

"I just want you to be careful. You have plenty of time for boyfriends," her mother said.

"I know. I told you he's not my boyfriend. I like him a little but that's all. I need to go find my portable phone charger. Jaycee's going to be here any minute."

"Don't forget to take a hoodie. It's going to be much colder once the sun goes all the way down."

"I know." Bella hurried off to her room and Rosa had to fight the urge to go after her and warn her again not to leave her friends.

"I hope I can make it through these teenage years," Carrie said, shaking her head.

"You can."

"All this talk of boys and learning to drive. She's growing up, isn't she?"

Rosa nodded, that bittersweet joy a heavy weight in her heart.

Chapter Seven

The barbecue was one of the most delightful evenings Wyatt had experienced in a while. He always enjoyed hanging out with his sister and considered his brother-in-law one of his closest friends. But having Rosa there, listening to her laugh with Carrie and Bella, tease Joe and trade corny jokes with Logan, somehow turned the night magical.

He tried to tell himself he was simply savoring the delight of good food and family. That didn't explain how the stars seemed to sparkle more brightly and the air smelled more sweet.

"Everything was delicious," he said to Carrie. "That cherry pie was divine. Did you try a new recipe?"

She shook her head. "No. I'm using the same one Grandma always made. She got it from Abigail Dandridge, actually. The cherries are just extra delicious this year, I think."

"That must be it."

"Looks like somebody is out for the count," Joe said, gesturing to their outdoor sofa, where Logan had curled up a little while ago.

Wyatt followed his gaze and found his son sound asleep under the blanket Carrie had brought out for him earlier, after the sun had gone down and the evening had turned chilly.

He wasn't completely surprised. Their day had been filled with activity and fun.

Love for his son washed over him. Logan was the greatest gift.

"Good thing he can sleep anywhere."

"He is very lucky," Rosa said. "Some nights, I cannot even sleep in my comfortable bed with cool sheets and soft music playing."

What was keeping her up at night? Did she also ache for something she didn't have?

"We're watching Logan for you tomorrow and you said you're going into work early, right?" Carrie asked.

He made a face. "Yeah. Sorry about that."

"You know it's no problem at all. But I've got a great idea. Why don't you just let Logan stay over here for the night? He can sleep in and so can we, since tomorrow is the official holiday and we don't have a single thing planned."

That did make sense, though Wyatt didn't like spending even a night away from his son.

"Are you sure?"

"Yes. If you want the truth, I would rather sleep in tomorrow, since I imagine we will be up late worrying until Bella gets home safely."

Rosa looked concerned. "I am sure she will be fine. Bella is a smart girl and she is with her friend Jaycee and Jaycee's parents. They will make sure she does not get into any trouble."

"Parents always worry. It's what we do." Carrie shrugged. "Intellectually, I know Bella will be fine. I'll still probably stay up, which means I'll be doubly glad not to have to get up at six a.m., when you come to drop off Logan."

"I didn't bring any clothes for him."

"He has as many clothes here as he probably does at Brambleberry House. We have everything he should need. Swimsuits, shorts and sweatshirts. Even extra socks. It will be great."

Seriously, what would he have done without his sister and her family over the last three years, when they had stepped in after Tori died to help him raise his son?

"That does seem like a good solution, then. I'll carry him into the guest room."

"Afraid we're going to leave him out here on the patio to sleep?" Joe teased.

Wyatt smiled. "He probably wouldn't care. The thing is, Logan would never even notice if it started raining."

Only after he and Rosa had helped clean up and he had carried a still-sleeping Logan and tucked him into the sewing room daybed did Wyatt realize one significant issue he had overlooked.

If his son stayed here, that meant he and Rosa would be walking home alone together.

He frowned, suddenly suspicious. Carrie had been awfully quick to suggest that Logan stay the night, hadn't she? Were her reasons really about convenience and sleeping in the next day, or was she trying to do some behind-the-scenes matchmaking again?

He gave his sister a swift look, remembering that conversation in the kitchen.

Her reasons didn't matter. The deed was done. He and Rosa were walking back to Brambleberry House together and he could do nothing about it.

A short time later, they left the house, with Rosa carrying the bag with the bowl she had brought, now empty and washed.

Why had he thought it was a good idea to walk here earlier? If he had driven, they could have been home in two minutes.

The walk wasn't far, only a few blocks, but there

was an intimacy to walking alone with Rosa that left him uncomfortable.

He hadn't noticed it at all on the walk to Carrie's house, probably because Logan had kept up a constant chatter. His son had provided a much-needed buffer.

"The night turned a little cooler, didn't it? That came on suddenly."

She had brought a sweater, which she had put on earlier. Even so, she shivered a little.

"Yes. And it looks as if the fog they've been talking about is finally moving in."

Tendrils of coastal fog stretched up from the beach, winding through the houses. It added to the strange, restless mood stealing over him like the fog creeping up the street.

He put it down to leaving his son back at his sister's house. Surely that's what it was, not anything to do with his growing feelings for Rosa.

"You were right—Logan can sleep through anything. I would not have believed it but he did not even open his eyes when you carried him to bed. Will he wake up confused in a strange place?"

"I don't think so. He's spent the better part of the past two months sleeping there, except for the few weeks we've been at Brambleberry House. He's probably as comfortable there as he is in his own bed. I, on the other hand, probably won't sleep at all."

She gave him a sideways look. "Why is that?"

He shrugged, wishing he hadn't said anything. "When I don't have Logan nearby, I feel like part of me is missing."

She looked touched. "He is a very sweet boy."

"You've been very kind to help him learn Spanish for his friend. I know you're busy. Please let me know if it becomes too much of a burden."

"Impossible," she declared. "I am always happy to speak Spanish with someone. Sometimes I worry I will forget the language of my birth."

He suddenly remembered the conversation he'd had with his sister about her. What had she been through, the reasons Carrie said she deserved to be happy?

"That fog is growing more thick. I hope it goes out again in the morning so the weather stays good for the rest of the holiday weekend. It is a busy time for my store."

"Don't you have better business if it starts to rain? I would have thought fewer people would want to sit at the beach when it's raining, so they're more inclined to go shopping instead."

"Sometimes. Or sometimes they decide since it's raining to take a drive down the coast to Lincoln City, or even farther down to some of the other lighthouses like Heceta Head."

"The police department is busy whether it's

raining or not. It seems like holiday weekends always bring out the worst in people."

"Do you like your job as a detective?" she asked as they turned onto the Brambleberry House road.

The question took him by surprise. Not many people asked him that. He pondered for a moment before answering, wanting to be as honest as possible.

"I like when I have the chance to help people. That doesn't always happen. The past few years have made me question my job choices. I've seen a lot of injustice and been frustrated by it. Attitudes are changing, I think. It's just taking longer than it should. At the end of the day, I hope I can say I've worked for victims and for justice."

She said nothing for several long moments. When she spoke, her voice was low. "I will always be grateful for the *policia*. My father is the sheriff and he saved my life and the lives of my friends."

She turned onto the walk of Brambleberry House as if her words hadn't landed between them like an errant firework.

After his first moment of shock, he quickly caught up with her. "How did he do that?"

In the moonlight, she looked as if she regretted saying anything at all. "It is a long story, and not a very nice one. I do not like to talk about it."

Wyatt wanted to point out that she had been the one to bring it up. He had the odd feeling Rosa wanted to tell him about her past, but was afraid of his reaction.

"Well, if you ever decide you're willing to share your story with me, I like to think I'm a pretty good listener."

"I have noticed this. That is probably a help in your line of work, when you are fighting crime."

"I hope so."

He knew he had to get up early for his shift the next morning, yet he didn't want the evening to end.

To his vast relief, she didn't seem in a hurry to go to inside, either. She stood looking at the big, graceful old house in the moonlight. It was mostly in darkness except for a light in the shared entry and two lights glowing on the second floor.

In the wispy coastal fog, it looked mysterious, intriguing, though not nearly as interesting as the people who lived inside.

"Looks like our neighbor is home."

Wyatt didn't miss the way Rosa looked protectively toward the second floor, where a shadow moved across the closed curtain.

"Yes. I think she and Addie planned a quiet evening."

"She doesn't go out much, I've noticed."

"Have you?"

As he expected, she didn't take the bait, so he

came right out and asked the question he had been wondering since he moved in.

"What is Jen's story? You can tell me, you know."

In the moonlight, he saw Rosa's features tighten. "I don't know what you mean."

She did. She knew perfectly well. "Why does she seem so nervous around me?"

"Nervous?"

"Yeah. She has allowed her little girl to play with Logan a few times, but Jen herself clearly goes out of her way to avoid me. I'm not sure she's ever looked me in the eye."

Rosa looked away herself. "Maybe she does not like policemen."

"Is she in some kind of trouble? Do you know?"

"Why would you ask that?" Her innocent-sounding question didn't fool him at all. She knew exactly what was going on with Jen.

"I can't help her if nobody will tell me what's going on," he pointed out mildly. He didn't want to intrude, but he was an officer of the law and his job was to protect and serve. That included those who shared the same house with him.

"She has work at the store and she has a safe place to live. That is good for now." She paused. "But thank you for being concerned for her."

"I'm here to help, if you or she ever want to tell me what's going on."

She nodded slowly. "I will tell her this."

"You know I'm one of the good guys, right? At least I try to be."

She gave him a long look in the moonlight. "Yes. I know. I would not have let you move in if I did not think that."

Her words made him feel as if he had passed some kind of test he had no idea he'd been taking.

He was suddenly glad that Carrie had encouraged him to take this apartment for the month, grateful for summer nights and lovely women.

Again, he felt an overwhelming urge to kiss her, this woman with secrets who was filled with so much compassion for those around her.

She didn't trust him. He looked at the house, hating the idea of his empty apartment and his empty bed and the loneliness that had been such a part of his life since Tori died.

"I should probably go in."

"Yes. You are working early tomorrow."

He nodded. "Thank you for the lovely evening. I enjoyed the walk home. I think maybe I've forgotten how much I enjoy talking with a woman."

She gazed at him, eyes wide. In the dim light of the moon, he saw her swallow and her gaze seemed to slide to his mouth.

The scent of her, sweet and feminine, with hints of vanilla and berries, drifted to him. He wanted to close his eyes and inhale her inside him.

"I am glad I could remind you of this," she finally said.

He knew he should walk away, turn around and go into the house, to that empty apartment and the even emptier bed. He couldn't seem to make his muscles cooperate. The pull of her was too strong and he had no tools to withstand this slow, aching desire churning through his blood.

"I would like to kiss you right now."

As soon as he heard the words, he wanted to call them back, but it was far too late. They danced between them like petals on the breeze.

He thought she would turn and walk away since he couldn't seem to do it. Instead, she only gazed up at him out of those soft brown eyes he wanted to sink into.

"Would you?" she finally asked, her voice soft and her accent more pronounced than usual.

"Yes. Would you mind?"

After a brief hesitation, as if she was debating with herself, she shook her head slightly.

That was all the encouragement he needed. He lowered his mouth to hers, his heart beating so loudly in his ears it almost drowned out the ever-present sound of the ocean.

If he had forgotten how much peace he could find talking with a woman, he had *really* forgotten how much he loved to kiss a woman in the moonlight.

Her mouth tasted of strawberries and cream, and her lips trembled slightly. She must have set down the bag she had been carrying because one hand grasped his shirtfront and the other slid around his neck.

It was the perfect moment, the perfect kiss. He had no other way to describe it. A light breeze stirred the air around them, the ocean murmured nearby and the moonlight played on her features.

He wanted to stay right here, with his heart pounding and her mouth soft and sweet and generously responding to his kiss.

Here, he could focus only on the perfection of this moment. Not on the pain of the past or the mysteries that surrounded her or all the reasons they could never have anything but this kiss.

Chapter Eight

In her secret dreams, Rosa had wondered before what it would be like to kiss Wyatt. Having him live downstairs from her these last few weeks had only increased her attraction to the man, so, of course, she would wonder.

She had suspected kissing him would be an unforgettable experience.

She had not expected it to knock her legs out from under her.

Rosa closed her eyes, her heart pounding as his mouth explored hers.

Now, as he kissed her, she could admit that she had been attracted to him for a long time. Long before he had moved to Brambleberry House, she had been nervous around him. She had told herself it was because of his position with the police department. Now she could admit it was because of the man himself.

His kiss staggered her.

Why? She had kissed other men, of course. Not counting the awful time in her youth that she didn't like to think about, she had had boyfriends.

She wanted to think she had a healthy relationship now with men, with sex, especially after the counseling her parents had insisted on.

She didn't blame all men for what had happened to her.

Even so, Rosa was fully aware that she usually gravitated toward a different sort of man. Someone who was not as masculine as Wyatt.

Those kind of men were the safer bet, she realized now. They didn't threaten her. She always had held most of the control in every other situation.

Not with Wyatt. Kissing him felt like being caught in a riptide, as if she were whirling and spinning from forces beyond her control.

Sometimes when she saw the intensity between Lauren and Daniel, or her aunt Anna and Harry, Rosa wondered if she had something fundamental broken inside her.

She had assumed that the scars she bore so deeply inside made it impossible for her to feel that kind of passion.

Kissing Wyatt in this moment made her question every single one of those foolish assumptions.

She could want, with a searing intensity that left her breathless.

She wanted to drag him to the dewy grass and kiss him for hours. And more. She wanted more with him.

And then what?

Cold, hard reality seemed to push through the dreamy haze that surrounded her.

After this kiss, then what? Try as she might, she couldn't envision a scenario where she and Wyatt could have anything but a few wild kisses. Where they could live happily ever after.

He was a police detective and she was…herself. A product of what had happened to her and the choices that had led her here to this moment.

They could never be together, so what was the point in setting herself up for more pain?

She drew in a breath, willing her hunger to subside. When she thought she had herself under control enough that she could think straight again, she slid her mouth away, cooled by the night air that swirled around them. After another inhalation, she made herself take a slight step back.

She couldn't see him clearly, but she could tell he had been as caught up in the kiss as she was.

He gazed down at her, his eyes slightly unfocused and his hair messy from her fingers. He looked so delicious, she had a hard time not stepping straight back into his arms.

She had to say something, but all the words seemed tangled up inside her like fishing line discarded on the beach, a jumble of Spanish and English that made no sense, even to her.

She finally swallowed hard and forced a smile.

"That was a surprise."

He continued to look down at her, his face so close she could see each distinct long eyelash and the fine network of lines etched into the corners of his eyes.

He released a long breath. "Yes. It was."

"I thought you meant a little good-night kiss like a friend would give a friend."

"That was substantially more, wasn't it?"

She could feel the imprint of his mouth on hers, could still taste him on her tongue—the wine and mint, the strawberries and cream from the dessert his sister had made. She shivered a little, wishing she could lean in for another kiss.

"Indeed." She hated this awkwardness between them, especially after the closeness they had shared on the walk from his sister's house. She shook her head.

"I'm sorry if I turned the kiss into more than you wanted."

"You didn't. That is the problem. I want, though I know I should not."

He gave a slightly raw-sounding laugh, as if startled by her honesty. "Same. I want. And I know I should not. What are we going to do about that?"

Rosa spent a delicious moment imagining what she would like to do. She wanted to drag him up two flights of stairs to her cozy bedroom under the eaves and spend the entire night exploring all his muscles and hard edges.

That was impossible, for a hundred reasons. The biggest one was right now at the house they had come from.

"I don't know what you will do, but I will go inside, take a soak in the tub and try to focus on something else."

A muscle worked along his jawline as if he was trying to keep himself from responding. He finally nodded. "I suppose that's for the best."

Rosa managed a smile, trying to pretend she wasn't fighting with everything inside her to keep from doing what she longed to do—tug him back into her arms and kiss him again until they both forgot all the shoulds and should nots.

"Good night to you, Wyatt. I enjoyed the evening...and the kiss."

"Rosa..." he began, but she didn't wait to hear what he said. She hurried up the steps, unlocked the front door with hands that trembled and rushed up to her apartment.

As she took the stairs quickly, she thought she

felt an odd cold spot on the stairs and had the strangest feeling that the house or its inhabitants were disappointed in her.

She and Wyatt had decided not to take the dogs with them because of Carrie's spoiled and rather unfriendly cats. Inside the apartment, Fiona rose to greet her, giving her an unblinking stare, as if she knew exactly what Rosa had just been doing in the moonlight with their downstairs neighbor.

"Not you, too."

Fi snorted as if she had plenty to say but only regretted that she did not have the words.

"What do you want me to do?" she said aloud to her dog. "You know I cannot invite the man up. He is a police officer. He would not be interested in me, if he knew the truth."

Fiona whined. She needed to go out, but Rosa wasn't eager to go down the stairs again and risk meeting up with Wyatt. Her dog's needs came first, though.

"Don't be like that," she said as she hooked up Fi's leash. "You know it is true. I have too many secrets I cannot tell him."

The dog didn't look convinced.

"I cannot," Rosa insisted. "You know I cannot. They are not only my secrets. I cannot tell him."

Wyatt was a good man, A decent, honorable man, she thought as she walked down the stairs again and outside into the moonlight. To her relief, she didn't see any sign of him.

He reminded her so much of Daniel, who would always be her hero for rescuing her in her darkest moment.

She loved her adopted father dearly so she supposed it was only natural that she would be so fiercely drawn to a man who had all of Daniel's best qualities.

"It doesn't matter," she said. She didn't feel foolish carrying on this conversation with her dog. Fiona was the best possible confidante, who listened to all her inner thoughts and only judged a little.

She didn't tell the dog that she suspected she might be falling for Wyatt, though she knew he would never feel the same. Not if he knew the truth.

She knew he was still grieving for his wife. Even if the two of them shared a few kisses, she knew Wyatt wasn't in a good place for anything more.

She wanted things to be different. If only they were both free of their pasts and had met under other circumstances. But she knew she wouldn't have been the same person without all that had happened to her and she thought the same of Wyatt.

She would not kiss him again. What would be

the point? Nothing could come of it and she would only end up with more pain.

With the Oregon coast in full tourist season, Rosa didn't have time to think about that kiss more than about two or three dozen times a day at random moments.

Over the next week, she made several day trips out of town to the central coast and to Portland to pick up inventory from some of their vendors.

Today she was busy revamping her window display a week after Independence Day, adding in the new products she had collected to feature, while Jen worked the cash register and assisted customers.

Rosa was thrilled at the change in her friend. Jen had come so far over the past few weeks. She was far more relaxed with the customers. She smiled and chatted easily and seemed to have lost that haunted look she used to wear at random moments.

"Thank you. Come back again. We have new inventory all the time," she told the final customer at her register. A few other browsers were looking at their selection of T-shirts, but they didn't seem in any hurry so Rosa left the window to walk over to Jen and check on her.

"How are things going?" she asked.

"Great. Really good." Jen smiled, looking far

more like the woman Rosa remembered from their college days together. "It's hard to be in a bad mood when the weather is so glorious, isn't it?"

They really had been blessed with unusually sunny weather. It was good now, but made her worry about forest fires later in the season.

"You seem to be more comfortable with the customers."

"I am enjoying the work, but to tell you the truth, I'm starting to miss teaching. This is the time of year when I would usually start thinking about my classroom decorations for the next school year and working on lesson plans."

Jen had been a third-grade teacher in Utah and had loved her career. That was one of the things that angered Rosa the most, that her friend had been forced to leave all that she loved in order to escape.

"I can understand that."

"I was actually wondering if I could take a day off tomorrow. I know it's short notice."

"Of course," Rosa said immediately. "I can re-arrange the schedule. If I cannot find anyone to cover for you, I will work myself. That should not be a problem, especially now that the holiday weekend is over."

"Thank you. You won't believe this but I al-ready have a job interview lined up!"

"Oh, that's wonderful!"

Rosa knew Jen had recently finished the process to certify her Utah teaching license in Oregon and that she had started applying in the area.

"The first school I contacted called me today and want to talk to me tomorrow. It's at Addie's school, which would be ideal."

"Oh, that is so exciting. Of course, you can have the day off. Or more than that, if you need it."

"To be honest, I'm not sure if I should apply. If I found a job, I would have to quit working here before the tourist season is over in September."

Rosa waved a hand. "Don't worry about that for a moment. I have temporary seasonal workers who have asked for more hours, so I can give them your shifts if you get a new teaching contract. I'm just happy that you like it enough here in Oregon to think about staying for a while."

Jen hugged her and Rosa was happy to note that she had started to gain weight again and seemed to have lost that frail, hunted look.

"It's all because of you," Jen said. "I can't thank you enough for all you've done since I moved here. Giving me this job, a place to live. You have been amazing."

Rosa was only happy she had been in a position to offer help.

"I have been grateful to have you and Addie here. You would have a job here at the store as long as you want, but it would be wonderful for you to return to teaching. You were made to be a teacher."

The T-shirt customers came over to ask a question, distracting them from further conversation. The door opened and more customers entered, so Rosa moved to help them.

A constant flow of traffic moved in and out of the store over the next few hours and she was too busy to have another chance to talk to her friend about her interview.

Finally, things seemed to slow near the end of Jen's shift. One of the other seasonal workers, Carol Hardesty, came in a little early for her own shift and Rosa was about to tell Jen to take off for the day when she suddenly heard a loud crash.

Rosa jerked up her head, instantly alert, to find Jen staring out the window, the shards of a broken coaster scattered at her feet.

Fortunately, it was a fairly inexpensive one in a design that hadn't been particularly attractive, anyway.

"Is everything okay?" she asked, when Jen continued to stare out the window.

Her words seemed to jolt the woman back to her senses. Jen looked down at the mess, a dawning look of horror on her features.

"Oh, no. I'm so sorry."

Rosa moved quickly to her. "You look frightened. Are you all right? Has something happened?"

"Yes. No. I don't know. I just… I thought I saw…"

"A ghost?" Carol hurried up with a broom and dustpan and started sweeping in her no-nonsense way. "We get those here in Cannon Beach. Once, I swear I saw a man all wrapped up in bandages walking around the side of Highway 101. When I slowed down to see if he needed help, he was completely gone. Spooky!"

"Yes. It must have been…something like that."

Jen looked like a ghost herself with her suddenly pale features.

"And the really creepy part is," Carol went on, "when I mentioned it to a few people, I found out Bandage Man is kind of a legend around here. There was even a stretch of the old highway called Bandage Man Road. Weird, right?"

Jen hardly seemed to hear her, still staring out the window.

"You need to sit down for a minute."

"Yes," Carol urged. "I've got this mess and I'll handle any customers. Don't worry about a thing."

Rosa guided a numb Jen to the back room she used as an office, which was also where most of the employees took their breaks. Jen sagged into a chair and Rosa crouched beside her, holding her hand.

"Who did you see? Was it the man you fear?"

Jen shook her head. "Not him. But maybe a friend of his. I can't be sure. I only caught a glimpse of him through the window, but I think he was looking at me as if he knew me."

Her panic was only too familiar to Rosa. She knew just how it felt to be hunted. The memories crowded into her mind but she pushed him away.

This was not about her. This was about Jen and her fear and the man who had made her life hell for months.

Rosa did not offer platitudes because she knew how useless they could be.

"What do you need? Do you want me to call the police? You know you can trust Wyatt. Detective Townsend. He is a good man."

For a moment, Jen looked as if she would consider doing just that, then she shook her head. "What would I say? That I think I might have seen a man who might be friends with a man who scares me but who has never actually touched me? He will think I'm crazy."

"He will not think you are crazy." Rosa did not know how she knew this so completely, but she had no doubt that Wyatt would take Jen's concerns seriously. "Stalking is against the law in Oregon, just as it was in Utah. I believe Wyatt will help you. He will want to know what you think you saw."

Again, Jen looked tempted. Rosa even pulled out her phone, but her friend finally shook her head firmly. "I'm imagining things. I'm sure of it.

It was only a man who looked like someone from our town. I don't want to bring Wyatt in."

"You know he will help."

"Yes. If there was anything he could do, but there's not. I cannot run from shadows for the rest of my life. Aaron would have no reason to know I'm here. He doesn't know one of my dearest friends lives here. I never mentioned you to him. And if it was his friend, he couldn't possibly recognize me. I don't look the same. I've lost thirty pounds, my hair is shorter and a different color. I have contacts now instead of glasses. He would have no reason to even connect Jen Ryan with the woman he knew as Jenna Haynes."

Rosa was still not convinced. She had heard the fear, the sheer terror in Jenna's voice when Rosa had called her. She thought it would just be a regular phone call to wish her a happy birthday. Instead, Jenna had spewed out such a story of horror that Rosa had been physically sick to her stomach.

"You must come here," she had told her college friend firmly in that phone call. "I have an empty apartment right now. Just bring Addie and come tonight."

"I can't drag you into this," Jen had replied through her tears. "You've been through enough."

"That is why I have to help you. You are my friend. I cannot let you live in fear if you do not have to. Come to Oregon, where this man does not know anyone. You will be safe here."

Jen had been desperate enough to escape her situation that she had finally agreed, leaving in the middle of the night with only their clothes.

She was finally beginning to relax and enjoy her life again. Rosa hated to think of her living in fear again.

"Please. Consider talking to Wyatt," she said now. "He knows something is wrong. He asked me about it the other night. You know he is a good man. He will do what he can to keep you safe."

"I'll think about it," Jen finally said. Color had returned and she seemed to be breathing more easily, Rosa was glad to see.

"Give me a moment and I will give you a ride home."

Worried that the man stalking her had put a trace on her vehicle, Jen had traded her car in the Boise area for an older model sedan that had seen better days. It was currently in the shop, where it had been for several days.

Jen shook her head. "No. Thank you, though. I would rather walk."

"Are you sure?"

"It's less than a mile and I can pick up Addie on the way. The walk will clear my head."

"Are you sure?"

Jen nodded. Her features grew soft. "I meant

what I said earlier. I cannot thank you enough for all you've done for me. You've given me hope that someday soon I will stop looking over my shoulder. I wish there was some way I could repay you."

"You have, a hundred times. I love seeing you take back your life. You and Addie deserve everything wonderful I know is in store for you."

Jen smiled, though traces of panic still lingered in her eyes. As soon as she left, Rosa almost picked up her phone and called Wyatt herself, but she decided against it. Jenna's story was her own. She had her reasons for keeping it to herself.

Rosa, who had plenty of secrets of her own, could not fault her for that, even though she knew Wyatt was the kind of man who would do everything he could to keep Jenna and Addie safe.

Chapter Nine

After leaving Carol and another of her part-time workers to close the store, Rosa returned to Brambleberry House tired, but in a strange, restless mood. She needed to bake something. The urge did not hit her very often, but when it did, she tried to go with it.

Baking reminded her of her mother. Maria Elena had been an amazing baker who used to make delicious delicacies she would sometimes sell in the market. Anything to make a few lempiras.

Rosa still liked making the treats of her childhood, but today she was feeling more like good old-fashioned chocolate-chip cookies, a treat she had come to love as a teenager.

She was just taking the first batch out of the oven when her phone rang. For a moment, she thought about ignoring it. Hardly anyone ever reached out to her with a phone call anymore, unless there was some kind of trouble. It might be Lauren, though, who still liked to have long chats on the phone since they couldn't connect as often in person.

Without looking at the caller ID, she tapped her earbud to answer the call as she slid the tray of cookies onto the cooling rack and put the next tray into the oven.

"Buenas," she said, distracted.

"Hello?" a male voice replied. "Is this Rosa Galvez?"

Her heartbeat accelerated as she recognized Wyatt.

Oh, this was so stupid. They had shared one kiss. Granted, it had been earthshaking for her, but that did not explain why she became weak in the knees, simply knowing he was on the other end of a telephone call.

She was tempted for a moment to tell him "no, wrong number," and disconnect the call. That would be childish, though. What was the point of hiding from the reality that she was falling for a completely inappropriate man?

"Sí. Yes. This is Rosa."

"*Hola*, Rosa. This is Wyatt Townsend. From downstairs."

As if she knew any other Wyatt Townsends who could make her head spin. "Yes. I know. Is everything all right?"

He sighed. "Not really. I have a little problem and was wondering if I could ask for your help."

The word shocked her. Wyatt was not the sort of man who could ask for help easily. "Of course. What do you need?"

"I just got called to cover an emergency and Carrie, Joe and Bella have gone to Portland. They're leaving for San Francisco from there. I'm in a bind and need someone to watch Logan for a few hours."

"Of course," she said instantly. "Fiona and I would be glad to help you. I can be down in ten minutes, as soon as I take some cookies out of the oven."

"You don't have to come down. I can bring him upstairs to you. He's used to sleeping on the couch."

"Don't be silly. He would be more comfortable in his own bed. We will be there in ten minutes."

She had more dough, but decided she could put it in the refrigerator for now and later freeze it for another day.

"Thank you. I appreciate that. Hopefully I won't be gone past midnight."

"Even if you are, I won't mind," she assured him. "I'll be down soon."

While she waited for the timer, she gathered her laptop and a small knitting project she had been working on. She also waited for the first batch of cookies to cool enough before transferring them to a plate to take downstairs with her. As soon as the timer went off, she turned off her oven, pulled out the cookie tray and transferred the cookies to another cooling rack, then headed down the stairs with Fiona following close behind her.

Wyatt opened the door before she could knock, as if he had been watching for her.

"I'm really sorry about this."

"Please do not apologize. I'm happy to do it."

"Logan is already in bed. He'll be sorry he missed you."

She was disappointed that she wouldn't have a chance to hang out with the sweet boy and teach him more Spanish words. She would have enjoyed reading him a story and tucking him in.

"Too bad. I brought him some cookies. Ah, well. He can have one when he wakes up."

"If I don't eat them all first. They look delicious."

He smiled and she had to remind herself she was here to watch his child, not to moon over the boy's father.

She did her best to ignore how fiercely she

wanted to kiss him again. It helped to focus on the gleaming badge he was wearing over the pocket of his sports coat, which reminded her of all the differences between them.

"Anything special I need to know or do?"

"Not really. Since the fire, Logan does have the occasional nightmare. If he has one, you only have to stay close and help talk him through it until he falls back asleep."

"Oh, *pobrecito*," she exclaimed.

His eyes seemed to soften. "Yeah. He's been through a few things. The nightmares are not as frequent as they were right after the fire. He probably won't even wake up but I wanted to warn you, just in case."

"Got it."

"Thank you again."

"Do not worry about things here. Go take care of what you have to do. I will be here. And take a cookie with you."

He grabbed one with a smile that left her feeling slightly light-headed. She told herself it was because she had only eaten a warm cookie for dinner.

After he left, she was again struck by how Wyatt and Logan had settled into the space. A video-game controller sat on the coffee table, along with a trio of plastic dinosaurs and several early-reader chapter books.

The house smelled like Wyatt, that combination

of scents she couldn't pinpoint. She only knew it reminded her of walking through a forest after a rainstorm.

A light was on next to the easy chair in the sunroom. She wandered in and found a mystery novel with a bookmark halfway through on the side table. A small bowl of popcorn sat next to it.

Rosa's own limited detective skills told her he must have been reading and enjoying a snack when he got the call from work. She liked thinking about him here, enjoying the sound of the ocean in the night through the screens.

While Fiona found a comfortable spot on the rug next to Hank, Rosa continued on her tour. She briefly went to the room she knew Logan used and opened the door a crack to check on him.

The boy was sleeping soundly, sprawled across the bed with a shoebox that looked like it contained treasures tucked nearby.

She fought the urge to go to him, to smooth away the hair falling into his eyes.

The night of the storm, Wyatt had said Logan was a sound sleeper, but she still didn't want to run the risk of waking him and having him be confused at finding her here and not his father.

She did, however, take a moment to adjust the blanket more solidly over his shoulders.

Oh, he was dear boy. Just looking at him made her smile. He looked a great deal like his father, but his lighter coloring and the shape of his nose must have come from his mother's side.

Rosa had to wonder about the woman. She had seen a picture of them all together at Carrie and Joe's house. She had been pretty, blonde, delicate-looking.

Carrie had told her Tori Townsend had been a talented artist and writer, in addition to a school guidance counselor. Though she had been a runner who regularly worked out, she had tragically died of a previously undiagnosed heart condition at a shockingly young age.

Logan must grieve for her terribly, she thought. *Both of them must.* It made her heart ache, thinking of this sweet boy growing up without his mother.

At least he had a father who doted on him and an aunt, uncle and cousin who showered love and affection on him, as well.

After she had assured herself Logan was sleeping comfortably, she returned to the living area. It felt strange to be here in Wyatt's space without him. She wasn't quite sure what to do with herself.

She finally turned on the audiobook she was listening to through her ear pods and picked up her knitting. While the dogs slept tangled together at her feet, she worked and listened to the audiobook above the sound of the wind in the trees and the ever-present song of the ocean.

The chair was comfortable and her day had

been long. Soon she gave in to the inevitable and closed her eyes, thinking she would only doze for a moment.

She had a dream she was running. It was cold, bitterly cold, and she was barefoot. She was so afraid, not only for herself. She had nowhere to go and the winter snow blew past her and through her. So cold. Always so cold. She had been used to sunshine and heat and could never seem to warm up here.

Everything hurt. Her face, her arms, her stomach where she had been kicked and beaten. She needed help but didn't know where to go.

And then she saw him. A police officer. She thought at first it was Daniel but as he came closer she saw it was Wyatt, looking down at her with concern.

"What happened? Why are you running?"

She shook her head, too afraid to tell him. What would he think if he knew? He would never look at her the same way.

"It does not matter," she told the dream Wyatt. "I must keep running. If I don't, they will find me."

"Who?"

"The ghosts," she told him. Tears were running down her face. She could feel them dripping down her cheeks and reached to brush one away but it dried before she could touch it.

"I will protect you. I'm with the *policia*. Just like Daniel. Trust me, Rosa. Trust me. Trust me."

As she watched, the fear still coursing through her with every heartbeat, his image grew more and more faint until he completely disappeared, leaving her alone again.

She awoke with gritty eyes, a dry mouth and the unsettling sensation that she was not alone.

Rosa blinked for a moment in the darkness, not sure exactly where she was. Not her bedroom in Brambleberry House. She would remember that. Not her room at her parents' home in Utah, either.

A man was there, she suddenly realized. She could see the outline of him in the darkness. She struggled up, tangled in yarn, as instinctive fear and dark memories crowded through her, leaving little room for rational thought.

She had to escape. Run. Hide.

A hand was suddenly on her arm. "Easy. It's okay. It's me."

The voice, calm and measured, seemed to pierce her sudden panic. She knew that voice. Wyatt Townsend.

Was this still part of her nightmare?

Not a nightmare. She blinked a little more as the room came into focus and her consciousness seemed to calibrate again. Right. She had been watching his son for him while he went out to a crime scene and she must have fallen asleep.

Rosa drew in a deep, shuddering breath, embarrassed that she had given in to unreasonable panic for a moment. She thought she had come too far for that.

"You startled me."

"I'm sorry. I didn't mean to. I was just debating if you would be more annoyed with me for waking you or for letting you sleep here until the morning."

"I am not annoyed with you," she assured him. "I was having a bad dream. I am glad you woke me from it."

"Do you mind if I turn on the lamp?"

She probably looked horrible, with her hair tangled and her eyes shadowed. She carefully reached a hand up to her cheek and was relieved when she didn't feel any moisture. The tears must have only been in her dream.

"It's fine. Go ahead."

He did, and that's when she saw the fatigue in his eyes. This was more than physical, she realized instinctively. Something was very wrong. She wasn't sure how she knew but there was an energy that seemed to be seething around him. Something dark and sad.

"What is it?" She could not resist asking, though

she wasn't sure she wanted to know the answer. "What has happened?"

He released a sigh that sounded heavy and tired. "It was a long, difficult night. That's all."

Whatever he had been dealing with seemed to have impacted him deeply.

She had seen that look before on her adopted father's face when he would return from a bad crime scene or accident. He would walk in the door and go immediately to Lauren, wherever she was, and would hold her tightly, as if she was his only safe haven in a terrible storm. She would hold him, comfort him, help him put the pieces of his soul back together before she sent him out again to help someone else.

She could not do that for Wyatt and it made her sad, suddenly. She was no one's safe haven.

"How can I help? Can I make you some tea?"

As soon as she made the offer, she thought it was silly to have even suggested it, but for some reason she thought something warm and comforting might be exactly what he needed to ease the turmoil.

He gave a ragged sound that wasn't quite a laugh. "I don't have any tea. And before you say you've got some upstairs and it will only take you a moment to run and get it, I'll tell you thank you but no. I probably need sleep more than anything.

And maybe one of your cookies, but I might save those for breakfast."

"Are you certain? I don't mind going to get tea."

He shook his head. "No. You have done more than enough. I'm sorry I kept you so late."

"What time is it?"

"Nearly two. I thought I would be back long before now but the case was…more complicated than I expected."

"I do not mind. I was glad to help."

"I'm deeply grateful to you for staying with Logan. Let's get you back home so you can at least spend a few hours in your own bed."

She rose, again fighting the urge to go to him, wrap her arms around his waist and let him lean on her for a moment.

"Did everything go okay with Logan?" he asked. "No nightmares?"

She'd had one but hadn't heard a peep out of the boy. "Yes. Just fine. I checked on him when I first arrived and he was sleeping soundly. He doesn't keep the blanket on, though, does he?"

"Not usually. Sometimes I go in three or four times a night to fix it. He rolls around like he's doing gymnastics in his sleep. Once when we went camping, I actually woke up with bruises on my rib cage from him kicking me in his sleep."

He was a good father who adored his child. She

could picture him checking on the boy and making sure he was warm in the night. It touched her heart.

"I cannot think you enough for coming down at the last minute and helping out. None of our usual babysitters were available. With Carrie and Joe out of town, I didn't know what else to do."

"I really did not mind. I was honored that you would ask. Please do not hesitate to ask me again."

"If I do, I'll try not to keep you up until the early hours of the morning."

She shrugged and slung her bag over her shoulder. "I slept more soundly here than I probably would have at home. Please do not worry."

He smiled a little at that, but she could tell his eyes were still hollowed. What had happened?

"Do you have everything? Can I carry something?"

She wanted to roll her eyes when she realized he really did intend to walk her upstairs. "I have told you before, it is only two flights of stairs. I think I will be fine by myself. Get some rest."

"I need to move a little bit after tonight."

She nodded, understanding that sentiment. After that terrible time, she had needed to take long walks with Lauren, finding peace and comfort and a sort of meditation in the rhythm and the movement.

"Do you...want to talk about what happened tonight?" she finally asked.

"You don't want to hear. It was ugly."

She couldn't help it. She rested a hand on his arm. "I am sorry, whatever it was," she said quietly. "I can tell you are upset. If you were not, if you did not care and did not let the ugly touch you, then you would not be the good man you are."

He gazed down at her hand, his features tortured. After a moment, he made a sound of distress, then he folded her into his arms and held on tight.

"Why are people so horrible to each other?" he said, his voice sounding raw and strained.

She had no answer. What could she say? It was the question that had haunted her for fifteen years. One she was quite certain she would never be able to answer.

She only held him tightly, as she had seen Lauren do for Daniel, and tried to give him a little of her strength. She wanted to whisper that she would not let him go, no matter what, but, of course, she could not say that. How foolish to think that she, Rosa Vallejo Galvez, could protect anyone from the storm.

"Sometimes they are horrible," she agreed finally. "I do not know why. I wish I did. But more often people are good. They try to help where they can. I try to focus on the helpers instead."

They stood in the front room of his apartment, holding each other as emotions seemed to pour out of him. He didn't make a sound, but every once in a while, she could feel his shoulders shake as if it was taking everything inside him to keep from breaking down.

"Most of the time, I'm fine," he finally said, his voice still strained. "I like to think I can handle just about anything. But this one was hard. So hard."

"Tell me," she murmured.

"It was a murder-suicide. A domestic. A father who had lost a custody fight because of drug use and mental illness. Instead of accepting the court ruling or trying to fix his problems so he could have visitation, he decided that if he couldn't have his son, the mother wouldn't, either. He shot the boy and then shot himself. The kid was only five. A kindergartener. Younger than Logan."

At the despair in his voice, her heart cracked apart. She could only imagine how excruciating it must have been for Wyatt, who did everything possible to make his son's world better, to witness this kind of a crime scene.

Aching for him, she could do nothing but tighten her arms around him. "I'm so very, very sorry," she murmured.

He clung to her for a long time, there in the apartment, and she felt invisible threads between them tighten. Finally, he eased away, looking embarrassed.

"I'm sorry. I didn't mean to lose it like that. I'm…not sure why I did."

She suspected he had no one to share this kind of pain with since his wife died, which made her heart ache all over again.

"You hold too much inside," she said softly. "It cannot be easy, what you deal with every day."

"Yeah. Sometimes." He studied her, his expression intense. "This helped. More than I can ever tell you."

"I am glad. So glad. If you have another bad night, you know where to find me. Everyone needs someone to hold them when the world seems dark and hard."

"Thank you."

"You are welcome, Wyatt."

Something flashed in his gaze, something hungry and fierce. "I love the way you say my name."

All of the breath seemed to leave her in a whoosh. She swallowed as an answering heat prickled across her skin. "I do not say it in any way that is special."

"It is. It's unlike the way anyone else says it. Don't get me wrong. You speak beautiful, fluent English. I wish I could speak Spanish as well as you speak English. But sometimes your native language comes through on certain words."

The heat seemed to spread across her chest and down her arms. "I am sorry."

"No. Don't ever apologize. I like it."

He looked embarrassed that he had said anything, even as the first hint of a smile lifted the edges of his mouth.

He liked the way she said his name. She couldn't hear anything different in her pronunciation, but she wasn't going to argue.

"Wyatt," she repeated with a smile. "If it makes some of the sadness leave from your eyes a little, I will say it again. Wyatt. Wyatt. Wyatt."

His smile widened, becoming almost full-fledged for a brief moment, and Rosa could feel those invisible threads go taut.

After a moment, his smile faded. "What am I going to do about you?" he murmured.

She swallowed again. A smart woman would leave this apartment right now, would turn and hurry up the stairs to the safety of her own place. "There is nothing to do. We are friends. Friends help each other. They lean on each other when they need help."

He gazed down at her, his expression one of both hunger and need. "Do friends think about kissing each other all the damn time?"

Chapter Ten

Wyatt knew he shouldn't have said the words.

As soon as they were out, he wanted a do-over. Not because they weren't true. God knows, they were. He thought about Rosa Galvez constantly. Since the last time they had kissed, thoughts of her seemed to pop into his head all the time. She was like a bright, beautiful flower bringing happiness to everyone around her.

He was no exception. Thinking about her made him smile. Since he was thinking about her all the time, he was also smiling more than he had done in years. He knew it was becoming a problem when even other police officers had remarked on it.

Not that he really had anything to smile about.

He and Rosa could not be together. Yeah, they had shared a brief, intense embrace. But that was the end of it.

If he could only get his brain to get with the program, he would be fine. But every single time he thought about her, he thought about kissing her. And every time he thought about kissing her, he tried to remind himself of all the reasons why it was not a good idea for him to kiss her again.

None of that stopped him from yearning. He wanted Rosa Galvez in his arms, in his bed, in his life.

In some ways, Wyatt felt as if he had been living in a state of suspended animation for the past three years, as if he had been frozen, like some glitch on one of Logan's video games, while the world went on around him.

It wasn't a good place, but it wasn't really terrible, either. He could still enjoy time with his son, with his sister and her family, with his friends.

He handled his day-to-day responsibilities, cared for Logan, managed to do a good job of clearing his caseload. But whenever he thought about what the future might hold for him, all he could see was a vast, empty void.

Nothing had been able to yank him out of that emptiness. Even when his house caught fire, he hadn't really been devastated, only annoyed at the inconvenience.

His own reaction had begun to trouble him. People had told him that a house fire was one of the most traumatic things that could happen to a person, but Wyatt had merely shrugged and moved into problem-solving mode. Where they would live, what he might change about the house as he was having crews work on the renovations.

Even something as dramatic as being displaced hadn't really bothered him.

He could see now that his reaction had been a self-protective mechanism. After Tori's shocking death and the vast grief that had consumed him, he had slipped into some kind of place where he did not let anything touch him deeply.

Now he felt as if kissing Rosa had somehow kicked him in the gut, jolting him off his axis— that safe, bland existence—and into a world where everything seemed more intense.

A few months ago, he would have felt sad about the crime scene he had dealt with earlier, but it wouldn't have left him feeling shattered.

He was beginning to feel things more deeply and wasn't at all sure he liked it. A big part of him wanted to go back to the safety of his inertia.

If kissing her once could jerk him into this weird place, maybe kissing her a second time would help set things back the way they were before.

Even as he thought it, he knew kissing her again was a stupid idea. That did not stop him from reaching for her, pulling her into his arms again and lowering his mouth to hers.

She made a small, surprised sound, but didn't pull away. If she had, he would have stopped instantly. Instead, her arms went around his neck again and she pressed against him. She kissed him back, her mouth soft, sweet, delicious.

As she parted her lips and touched him tentatively with her tongue, he went a little crazy, all the raw emotions of the evening consolidating into one, his wild need for Rosa Galvez.

He deepened the kiss, his mouth firm and demanding on hers. He had to be closer to her. To touch her, to feel her against him.

She said his name again with that sweet little accented pronunciation, this time in a voice that was throaty and aroused.

He wanted to absorb it inside him.

He wanted to lose himself inside *her*.

His body ached with it, suddenly, the need he had shoved down for so long. He wanted to make love to Rosa Galvez right here in his living room. To capture her gasps and sighs with his mouth, to see her shatter apart in his arms.

Her breasts were pressed against him and he wanted more. He wanted to see her, to taste her. He reached beneath the hem of her shirt, to the warm, sweet-smelling skin beneath.

She shivered. The movement rippled over his fingers and brought him to his senses.

What the hell was wrong with him?

This woman had just spent hours sleeping in his easy chair to help him with his son and he repaid her by groping her in his front room?

He couldn't seem to catch his breath, but he did his best as he dropped his arms from around her.

She was breathing hard, too, her hair loose from the messy bun she had been wearing. She gazed at him out of eyes that looked huge and impossibly dark.

She had been so sweet to him, so comforting and warm when he needed it most. He had been at the lowest point he could remember in a long time and she had held him and lifted him out of it. In return, he had let his hunger for her overwhelm all his common sense.

"I'm sorry," he said, his voice ragged. "I don't know what happened there."

"Do not apologize." Her voice wobbled a little bit.

"Are you...okay? I didn't hurt you, did I?"

Her gaze narrowed, as if he had offended her somehow. "You only kissed me. I am not like some glass figure in my store falling off the shelf. I cannot be broken by a kiss, Wyatt."

There was his name again. It seemed to slide under his skin, burrowing somewhere in his chest.

What was he going to do about her?

Nothing, he told himself again. He just had to suck it up and forget about the way her kisses made him feel alive for the first time in years.

"I'll walk you upstairs."

She didn't argue, much to his relief. She only turned away, gathered her things and called to Fiona, then she and her dog hurried up the stairs.

Wyatt caught up with them on the second landing. The dog seemed to give him a baleful look, but he thought maybe that was just a trick of the low lighting out here in the stairway.

At her apartment, Rosa unlocked the door and opened it. "Good night."

Before he could thank her again for helping him out with Logan, she slipped inside and closed the door firmly behind her.

Wyatt stood for a moment, staring at the beautiful woodwork on the door, a match to his own two floors below.

That was as clear a dismissal as he could imagine. She had literally shut the door in his face.

He couldn't blame her. It was now nearly three and he knew she had to open the store early the next day, just as he had another shift.

He turned and headed down the stairs. He gripped the railing and told himself the shakiness in his legs was only exhaustion.

Something told him it was more than that. That

kiss had just about knocked his legs right out from under him.

He was falling for her.

The reality of it seemed to hit him out of nowhere and he nearly stumbled down the last few steps as if the fabled ghost of Brambleberry House had given him a hard shove.

No. He couldn't be falling for Rosa. Or for anyone else, for that matter.

He didn't *want* to fall in love again. He had been through that with Tori. Once was enough, thanks all the same. These feelings growing inside him were only attraction, not love. Big difference.

Yes, he liked her. She was sweet, compassionate, kind. And, okay, he thought about her all the time. That wasn't love. Infatuation, maybe.

He wouldn't let it be love.

The next day, Rosa was deadheading flowers in one of the gardens when Jen drove up in her rickety car, now running but not exactly smoothly. It shimmied a little as it idled, then she turned off the engine.

Rosa waved and Jen and Addie walked over.

"Hello, there," Rosa said. "How did the interviews go?"

"Good. Great, actually. The school offered me a job on the spot."

"Oh, that's terrific! We should celebrate. Have you eaten?"

"Yes. Sorry. Addie wanted a Happy Meal today."

"No problem. Maybe we can celebrate later. I have a bottle I've been saving for something special."

"It's a deal, as long as it goes with your famous chocolate-chip cookies."

Rosa had to smile. She had taken a plate down before she headed to the store and left them outside Jen's front door.

"Can we help you with the gardening?"

"Yes. Of course. That would be great. Thank you."

Addie frowned. "Why are you pulling all the flowers, Rosa? That's naughty. My mommy says I can't pick the flowers or they die."

She smiled, charmed by the girl even as she felt a little ache in her heart. "I am not picking *all* the flowers. Only the ones that have finished blooming and have started to die. This way the flower plant has more energy to make new blossoms. You can help, if you want to. You just pop off the flower if it's brown or the petals have come off and put it in the bucket there."

"I can do that!"

Addie began the task, humming a little as she worked, which made Rosa smile.

"I have a confession," Jen said after a few moments. "After my interview, I probably could have come in and worked this afternoon. Instead, I picked up Addie from day care early and we played hooky for most of the afternoon."

"Good for you," Rosa said, feeling a twinge of envy. "Did you do something fun?"

"Yes. It was wonderful. We made a huge sand-castle and then played in the water a bit, then took a hike around the state park near Arch Cape."

"Oh, I love that area. It is so beautiful and green, like walking through a movie, with all the ferns and moss."

"Yes. Addie thought it looked like a fairy land."

Oh, Addie was cute. She had such an innocent sweetness about her. Rosa hoped she could keep it forever.

"So," Jen said after a moment. "You and Detective Gorgeous. Is that a thing now?"

Rosa, yanking out a nasty weed that had dug its roots in deep, almost lost her balance.

She could feel her face grow hot. "Why would you say such a thing?"

"I *might* have heard two people going up the stairs together in the early hours of the morning."

Rosa could only be grateful they had kissed in his apartment and not in the stairway for her friend to overhear.

"So are you two…dating or something?"

She had a sudden fervent wish that she could

say yes. The idea of doing something as ordinary and sweet as dating Wyatt seemed wonderful but completely out of reach.

"No. We are not dating. Only friends." *Who kiss each other as if we can't get enough*, she wanted to add, but, of course, she couldn't say that to Jen.

"He needed someone to watch his son last night while he went out on an emergency police call. His sister is out of town and he did not have anyone else to ask. It was an easy thing for me to help him."

Jen made a face. "Too bad. I was thinking how cute you two would be together. And it's obvious his son likes you."

Rosa could feel herself flush. She was coming to adore both Townsend males, entirely too much. "I am not interested in dating anyone right now." *No matter how gorgeous.*

Jen nodded and carefully plucked away at a rose that had bloomed past its prime. "I totally understand that and feel the same way. I'm not sure I'll ever date again."

Her emphatic tone made Rosa sad. Jen had so much love inside her to give. It was a shame that one bad experience had soured her so much on men.

"Your husband, he was a good man, yes?" Jen and her husband had met after college and Rosa had only met him at their wedding, and the few times they had socialized afterward, before she moved to Oregon.

"Oh, yes," Jen said softly. "Ryan was wonderful. After he died, I never thought I would find anyone again."

She plucked harder at the rose bush. "I wish I hadn't ever entertained the idea of dating again. I obviously don't pick well."

Rosa frowned. "You did well with your husband. Nothing else that happened to you is your fault. I wish I could help you see that. You had no way of knowing things would turn out like they have."

"That's what I tell myself," Jen said quietly. "Most of the time I believe it. In the middle of the night when I think about everything, it's harder to convince myself."

"You did nothing wrong," Rosa repeated in a low voice so that Addie didn't overhear. "You went on three dates with this man then tried to stop dating him when you began to see warning signs. You had no way of knowing he would become obsessive."

Jen sighed. "I still wish I could go back and do everything over again. I wish I had said no the very first time he asked me out."

"I know. I am sorry."

Rosa became angry all over again every time

she thought about how one man's arrogance and refusal to accept rejection had forced Jen to flee her life and live in fear.

She was so glad her friend seemed to be trying to put the past behind her and make plans for the future.

"And while I don't think I am the best judge of character right now and don't seem to pick well for myself, I do like Detective Townsend. He seems very kind and he is a wonderful father."

Rosa could not disagree. She felt a little ache in her heart at the reminder that she and Wyatt could not be together. Soon, he and his son would be moving out of Brambleberry House.

"He is a good man and, I think, cares very much about helping people."

She paused, compelled to press the situation. "He would help you, you know. You should tell him what is going on."

"I don't know about that."

"I do. Wyatt is a man you can trust. While he is living here, he can look around for anything unusual. Like having security on site."

"I suppose it is a little like that."

Rosa nodded. "That is one of the reasons I agreed to let him move in. I was worried about you and thought it might make you more comfortable to know he is only downstairs."

Jen gave her a sidelong look. "You mean it wasn't because of those beautiful blue eyes?" she teased.

Rosa flushed and tried to pretend she was inordinately fascinated with clipping back a climbing vine. "Does he have blue eyes? I do not believe I had noticed."

Jen snorted a little, which made Rosa smile. She was happy to be a subject of teasing if it could bring a smile to Jen's face.

"You said you're not interested in dating. Why is that?"

"I date," Rosa protested. "I went out three weeks ago to a concert down in Lincoln City."

"With a seventy-five-year-old widower who had an extra ticket."

"Mr. Harris is very sweet. And also lonely, since he lost his wife."

"You know you don't have to take care of everyone else in town. You should save a little of your energy for going after what you want."

If only it could be that easy. She knew what she wanted. She also knew she could not have it.

She didn't have a chance to answer before a vehicle pulled into the driveway. She stood up, suddenly breathless when she recognized Wyatt's SUV. She had not seen him since that emotional, passionate kiss the night before and wasn't sure how to act around him.

He climbed out, and a moment later opened the back door for his son, who hopped out and raced over to them.

"Logan! Hi, Logan!" Addie made a beeline for the boy, who waved at her.

"Hi, Addie. Your hands are muddy."

"I'm picking flowers. Rosa said I could, to help the other flowers grow better."

"Remember, you should only pick the flowers when a grown-up tells you it's okay," Jen said.

She looked momentarily worried, as if afraid Addie would wander through the entire beautiful gardens of the house pulling up the flowers willy-nilly.

"I want to help pick flowers. Can I?" Logan asked Rosa.

"You will have to ask your father if he does not mind."

The father in question drew nearer and she felt tension and awareness stretch between them. He gave her a wary smile, as if he didn't quite know how to act this evening, either. Seeing his unease helped her relax a little.

Yes, they had shared an intense, emotional kiss. That didn't mean things had to be awkward between them.

"Can I pick flowers?" Logan asked Wyatt. "Rosa said it's okay."

"We are taking away the dead and dying flowers to make room for new growth," she told him.

"I want to help, too," Logan said.

"Fine with me. As long as you do what Rosa says."

"Not a bad philosophy for life in general," Jen said, which made Rosa roll her eyes. She wasn't handling her own life so perfectly right now. Not when she was in danger of making a fool of herself over Wyatt.

"Is there something I can do to help?" Wyatt asked. "Were you trying to hang this bird feeder?"

She followed his gaze to the feeder she had left near the sidewalk.

"Yes. It fell down during the wind we had the other night. I was going to get the ladder and hang it back up."

"That would be a good job for Logan and me. Let me put our groceries away and I'll be right back out to do that for you."

"I'm sure you have enough to do at your house. You don't need to help me with my chores."

"Hanging a birdhouse is the least I can do after you pinch-hit for me last night with Logan."

To Rosa's dismay, she felt her face heat again.

Oh, she was grateful her blushes were not very noticeable. She felt as red as those roses.

She couldn't seem to help it, especially when all she could think about was being in his arms the night before, his mouth on hers, and the way he had clung to her.

Something seemed to have shifted between them, as if they had crossed some sort of emotional line.

She, Jen and the children continued clearing out the flower garden and moved to another one outside the bay window of Logan's room.

A few moments later, Wyatt came out of the house. He had changed out of his work slacks, jacket and tie into jeans and a T-shirt that seemed to highlight his strong chest and broad shoulders.

"Is the ladder in the shed?" he asked.

"Yes. It should be open."

"Come help me, Logan. You, too, Addie. This might be a job for three of us."

She watched them go to the shed and a moment later Wyatt emerged carrying the ladder mostly by himself, with each of the children holding tightly to it as if they were actually bearing some of the weight, which she knew they were not.

"He's really great with kids," Jen murmured.

Maybe so. That didn't make him great for *Rosa*.

It did not take him long to rehang the birdhouse

in the tree she pointed out. While she would have liked to hang it higher up on the tree, on a more stable branch, she knew she would not be able to refill the feeder easily without pulling out a ladder each time.

After Wyatt and his little crew returned the ladder to the shed, they came back out and she set them to work helping her clear out the rest of the weeds and dead blossoms in the garden.

Her back was beginning to ache from the repetitive motion, but Rosa would not have traded this moment for anything. There was something so peaceful in working together on a summer evening with the air sweet from the scent of flowers and the sun beginning to slide into the ocean.

"So how did you two meet?" Wyatt asked them.

"College," Jen replied promptly. "We were assigned as roommates our very first day and became best friends after that."

Both of them had been apprehensive first-year college students. Rosa had been quite certain she was in over her head. She had only been speaking English for three years. She hadn't known how she would make it through college classes. But Jen had instantly taken her under her wing with kindness and support.

She owed her a huge debt that she knew she could never repay.

"Here you are, living as roommates again, of a sort," Wyatt said casually.

"Yes," Jen answered. "Isn't it funny how life works sometimes? I was looking for a change and Rosa had an empty apartment. It worked out for both of us."

Wyatt looked at the children, now playing happily on the tree swing. "What about Addie's father? Is he in the picture?"

Jen gazed down at the flowers, grief washing across her features. "Unfortunately, no. He died two years ago of cancer. Melanoma."

"I'm sorry," Wyatt said gently.

He knew what it was to lose someone, too, Rosa thought. In fact, the two of them would be perfect for each other. So why did the idea of them together make her heart hurt?

Jen sighed and rose to face him. "I might as well tell you, Jen Ryan is not really my name."

Rosa held her breath, shocked that her friend had blurted the truth out of nowhere like that. She could tell Wyatt was shocked, as well, though he did his best to hide it.

"Isn't it?"

"Well, it's not wholly a lie. My name is Jenna Michelle Haynes. Ryan was my late husband's name."

He studied her. "Are you using his name for your surname now as some kind of homage?"

"No." She looked at Rosa as if asking for help, then straightened her shoulders and faced Wyatt. Rosa could see her hands clenching and unclench- ing with nerves. "Actually, if you want the truth, I'm hiding from a man."

Chapter Eleven

Wyatt stared, shocked that she had told him, though not really by what she said.

He had suspected as much, judging by her nervous behavior and the way Rosa was so protective of her. He just didn't know the details.

He suddenly felt as protective of her as Rosa did. Who would want to hurt this fragile woman and her darling little girl?

He immediately went into police mode. "Who is he? Can you tell me? And what did he do to make you so afraid?"

She sighed and looked at the children, who were laughing in the fading sunshine as Logan pushed

Addie on the swings. The scene seemed innocent and sweet, completely incongruous to anything ugly and terrifying.

She swallowed hard and couldn't seem to find the words until Rosa moved closer, placing a supportive arm through hers. Jen gave her a look of gratitude before facing him again.

"His name is Aaron Barker. He's also a police officer in the small Utah town where I was living after my husband died. He... We went out three times. Three dates. That's all."

Rosa squeezed her arm and Jen gripped her hand. One of the hardest parts of his job was making people relive their worst moments. It never seemed to get easier. He didn't want to make her rehash all the details, but he couldn't help her if he didn't know what had happened.

She seemed to sense that because after a moment, she went on. "Aaron was very nice at first. Showering me with affection, gifts, food. Sending flowers to the school where I taught. I was flattered. I was lonely and—and I liked him. But then he started pushing me too hard, already talking about marriage. After three dates."

She shook her head. "I finally had to tell him he was moving too fast for me and that I didn't think I was ready to start dating again."

Her voice seemed to trail off and she shivered a little, though the evening was warm. He didn't like the direction this story was taking. It had to be grim to send her fleeing from her home to Oregon.

"What happened?"

"He wouldn't take no for an answer. He kept asking me out, kept bringing me gifts. I finally had to be firm and tell him we weren't a good match and I wasn't going to change my mind. I thought he understood, but then he started driving past in his squad car at all hours of the day and night. He kept calling and texting, sometimes dozens of times a day. I had to turn my phone off. I went out to dinner one day with another teacher, a coworker and friend who happens to be a man. Nothing romantic, just friends, but that night Aaron sent me a long, vitriolic email, calling me a whore, saying if he couldn't have me, no one could, and all kinds of other terrifying things. I knew he must have been watching me."

"Why didn't you report him to the police?"

"I tried but this was a small town. The police chief was his uncle, who wouldn't listen to me. He wouldn't even take my complaint. I tried to go to the county sheriff's department but they said it was a personnel issue for our town's police department. I think they just didn't want to bother and didn't want to upset Aaron's uncle."

Again, Wyatt had to fight down his anger. He knew how insular small-town police departments and their surrounding jurisdictions sometimes could be. Often, police officers for one agency didn't want to get other agency police officers in trouble.

He had also been involved in stalking investigations and knew just how difficult the perpetrators could be to prosecute. Most laws were weak and ineffective, leaving the victim virtually powerless to stop what could be years of torture.

"This went on for months," Jen said. "I can't explain how emotionally draining it was to be always afraid."

Rosa made a small sound, her features distressed. He sensed she was upset for her friend but had to wonder if there was something else behind her reaction. Why wouldn't she tell him her secrets, like Jen was finally doing?

"I understand," Wyatt said quietly. "I have worked these kinds of cases before. I know how tough they can be on the victims."

"Aaron was relentless. Completely relentless. I changed my number, my email, closed down my social-media accounts, but he would find a new way to reach me. He…started making threats. Veiled at first and then more overt. When he mentioned Addie in one of his messages, I quit my teaching job and moved closer to my sister, about an hour away, but the night after I moved, my tires were slashed. Somehow he found me anyway."

So things had taken an even uglier turn. Wyatt wasn't surprised.

"How did you end up here?"

"Rosa happened to reach out to me out of the blue, right in the middle of everything. We hadn't talked in a while and she was just checking up on me. Calling to wish me a happy birthday. I didn't want to tell her, but everything just gushed out and I finally told her everything that had been going on."

She squeezed Rosa's arm. "I don't know what I would have done without her. I was telling her that tonight. She invited me to come stay with her here for a while. She offered me a job and an apartment. It seemed perfect, and honestly, I didn't know what else to do."

"I only wish I had known earlier what was happening to you," Rosa said, looking guilty. "I should have called you sooner."

"Don't ever think that. You reached out right when I was at my lowest point and offered me a chance to escape."

Jen turned back to Wyatt. "I packed up what we had and drove as far as Boise. Maybe I watch too much *Dateline*, but I traded my car on the spot at a used-car lot, in case Aaron had put some kind of tracker on my vehicle, then I drove here."

"That was smart."

"I don't know about that. I had a nice little late-model SUV with four-wheel drive that was great for the Utah winters. Now I've got a junker. It was probably the best swap the dealer ever made. But it got us here to Brambleberry House, where I have felt safe for the first time in months."

"I am so glad," Rosa said.

"I can't tell you how nice it has been not to constantly look over my shoulder."

"Do you think he's given up?" Wyatt hated to ask but didn't have a choice.

Her expression twisted with distress. "I want to think so. I hope so. But I don't know. I don't know how to find out without possibly revealing my new location."

"He was obsessed," Rosa said, placing a protective arm around her friend. "Jenna is only telling you a small portion of the things this man has done to her."

Wyatt hoped the man had given up, though he worried that by fleeing, she had only stoked his unhealthy obsession.

Moving several states away might not be enough to escape a determined stalker, especially not one with law-enforcement experience.

"Thank you for telling me this. I know it wasn't easy, but you've done the right thing. I'll do what I can to help you. You said his name is Aaron Barker?"

"That's right."

"Do you have a picture or description?"

"Yes. I can email you a picture and also link you to his social media."

"Texting me is better. He might have hacked into your email."

"He's done that before but I changed my account and password."

That might not be the deterrent she hoped. Someone determined enough could find ways around just about anything.

"Once you get me a picture of him and a description, I'll pass it around to other officers in the local PD and sheriff's department so we can be on the lookout. You're in Cannon Beach now and we take care of our own."

"Thank you." Jen looked overwhelmed to have someone else on her side. He understood. Victims of stalking could feel so isolated and alone, certain no one else would understand or even believe them and that their ordeal would never end.

"You're welcome."

He glanced at Rosa and found her looking at him with such warmth and approval that he couldn't seem to look away.

Addie came running over, with Logan close behind.

"Mommy," she said, tugging on Jen's shirt, "I have to go to the bathroom."

Jen gave her a distracted look then seemed to

sharpen her focus on her child. "Right. The door is locked. I'll get it for you."

She turned back to Wyatt. "Thank you," she said again. "I'll get you that picture."

"That's the best thing you can do right now."

"I'm glad I told you. Rosa was right."

She gave Rosa a look he couldn't quite interpret, but one that left him feeling as if he had missed something significant, and then Jen grabbed her daughter's hand and hurried for the house.

After she left, Wyatt turned to Rosa and found her looking at him with that same expression of warmth and approval.

"What were you right about?" he asked.

She shrugged. "I told her she could trust you. That you would help her if you could."

If she believed that, why wouldn't she trust him herself?

He could not ask. "I don't know how much I can do. I hope she's right, that he has lost interest."

"But you do not think so."

He couldn't lie. "If the man was willing to break the law to hack into her emails and completely disrupt her life to that extent, I can't see him giving up easily. I think he will keep searching until he finds her."

"What can we do?"

"Not a great deal unless he does something overt. I'm sorry."

"I feel so helpless."

"I know. It's a terrible feeling. I'll do a little internet sleuthing and see what I can dig up on the guy without coming right out and contacting his department. I don't want to run the risk of him getting wind that a detective in Oregon is looking into him, or that will certainly clue him in that she's here. Meanwhile, I'll circulate the picture around here when she gives me one and we will keep our eyes open."

It didn't sound like much, even to Wyatt. He hated that he couldn't do more. If this Aaron Barker was obsessed enough about Jenna and Addie, he would figure out a way to find them.

"Why can't some men take no for an answer?" she asked quietly.

He gave her a searching look but she quickly shifted her gaze away.

"It usually has to do with power and control. And some men just can't accept rejection."

"She has already been through so much, losing the man she loved with all her heart. It is not fair."

"No. It's not. I hate when any man hurts or threatens a woman, but I especially hate when he's in law enforcement."

"Thank you for believing her. That was the most important thing. Everyone else she told thought she was making it up to get attention or to get this man in trouble."

"You believed her."

"I know fear when I see it," Rosa said simply. "She is afraid or she would not have taken her daughter away from her family and her friends."

Something told him Rosa knew plenty about fear, as well. He wanted to press her to tell him but held his tongue.

"Have you had dinner?" he asked instead. "We were about to order takeout from the Thai place in town. Buying you dinner is the least I can do for your help last night."

She looked shocked by the invitation. For a moment, he thought she was about to say yes. She looked at Logan, who was now digging in the dirt nearby, with a softness in her eyes that touched him deeply.

After a moment, she looked back at Wyatt, her expression shielded again.

"No, thank you."

He wasn't expecting the outright rejection and didn't know what to say for a few seconds. "If you don't like Thai food, there's a good Indian place with fabulous curry that just opened on the other side of town. I've heard they deliver, too. Or we can hit up the trusty taco truck down the beach."

"I like Thai food," she said, her voice low.

He gazed at her, confused. Was it *him* she didn't like? "Have you already eaten, then?"

She shook her head. "No. I'm not really hungry and I have much work to do tonight."

"We can help you after we grab dinner," he suggested.

After a moment, she sighed, looking distressed again. "I...think it is best if we do not spend a great deal of time together."

"Why not?" He was either being particularly dense or she was being obtuse. "I thought we were friends. That's what you said last night."

"Yes. And then you kissed me and I forgot about being friends and...wanted more."

He felt his face heat up. He could be such an idiot sometimes. Did he really think they could go back to a casual friendship after he had basically had a breakdown in her arms the night before, and then kissed her with all the pent-up loneliness and need inside him?

"Neither of us is looking for romance right now," Rosa went on, deliberately looking away from him. "I know this. But when you kiss me, I forget."

He did, too. When he kissed her, when he felt her arms around him and her soft mouth under his and the curves he longed to explore, Wyatt wanted to forget everything and get lost in the wonder and magic of holding her.

Rosa was right. Neither of them was looking for romance. The more time they spent together, the harder it was becoming for him to remember that.

It would be better to keep their distance until his house was fixed, when he and Logan would move out. Once things were back to normal and he didn't run the risk of bumping into her every time he came home, they would be able to go back to their regular lives.

No more moonlit kisses on the stairway, no more quiet talks on the front porch of Brambleberry House.

Just him and his son and his work.

The future seemed to stretch out ahead of him, gray as a January day.

What if he was beginning to want more?

Chapter Twelve

A week later, he stood at his sister's kitchen sink, helping Carrie thread vegetables onto skewers for the grill.

"Thanks for having us for dinner. I've been so busy, I haven't had much time to cook and I think Logan is getting a little tired of the taco truck for dinner."

Carrie laughed. "Surely not. Who could be tired of that?"

He impaled a yellow squash on the metal skewer, followed by a mushroom and then a slice of onion. "I feel like I haven't seen you since the Fourth. Tell me all about your trip."

After taking Bella to the concert in Portland a week earlier, Joe and Carrie had driven down to San Francisco for a few days with her.

"It was fun. We did all the touristy things. Alcatraz, riding a cable car, going to Fisherman's Wharf. And, of course, shopping. You can't visit San Francisco without spending too much money. We bought some cute school clothes for the new year."

He needed to start thinking about the new school year. Logan would be starting second grade. Wyatt still had a hard time believing he was that old.

He was finishing the last of the skewers while Carrie did some shrimp and some chicken when the doorbell rang.

"Are you expecting someone else?"

His sister somehow managed to look coy. "Sounds like Bella is getting it. That will be Rosa."

He nearly impaled his finger instead of a mushroom. "Rosa is coming to dinner, as well?"

He had been trying to stay away from her the past week, at her request. How the hell was he supposed to do that when his sister invited them both over for dinner?

"Yes. I happened to drop into her store today and mentioned Joe was going to grill tonight, and we had plenty. She seemed a little down and I thought it might cheer her up a bit. I hope you don't mind."

Why was she down? He wanted to rush out and ask if she was all right but made himself stay put.

"And you didn't think to tell me until now that she was coming?"

"Does it matter?"

Yes. Most certainly. He would have refused Carrie's last-minute invitation if he had known the dinner party included a woman who had specifically told him they should avoid spending more time together.

"I just wish you had told me."

Carrie made a face. "I'm sorry. I just thought one more person for dinner wouldn't make a difference."

He frowned. This was the second time in only a few weeks that Carrie had invited them both over for a meal at the same time. That couldn't be a coincidence, could it? She had already mentioned she thought he should think about dating her friend.

Did his sister suspect he was beginning to have feelings for Rosa?

If Carrie had any idea about the attraction that simmered between them, Wyatt knew she wouldn't hesitate to do whatever she could to push them together as much as possible. She wouldn't be subtle about it, either.

He wanted to say something but before he

could, Rosa and Bella came into the kitchen, Bella chattering a mile a minute about their trip.

Rosa didn't seem to notice him at first. She was listening intently to Bella's story about the ghost tour they went on, and smiling at the girl's animation.

The two of them shared similar coloring. The same dark hair and dark eyes. With their heads together like that, they looked as if they could be sisters, catching up after a long time away.

He frowned suddenly as a crazy thought flitted across his brain. No. Impossible. He pushed it away just as Rosa lifted her head and caught sight of him.

Her eyes widened with shock. "Oh. Wyatt. Hello. I did not know you would be here."

If she had known, he had a feeling she would have refused his sister's invitation. Well, they were both here. Might as well make the best of it.

"Hi," he answered, just as Logan came in from the family room, where he had been playing a video game with Joe.

He, at least, looked thrilled about the other dinner guest.

"Rosa! Hi, Rosa!" he exclaimed. He rushed to her and wrapped his arms around her waist as if he hadn't seen her for months.

It had only been a few nights ago when he had gone up to her apartment for another Spanish lesson and had come back down naming every single kind of fruit they had in their house in Spanish.

"Buenas," she said to him. "How are you tonight?"

"I'm good. Guess what? We're having *piña* and *fresas* tonight."

"Delicious. Pineapple and strawberries. My favorite."

"I didn't know strawberries were *fresas*. I don't think I learned that in Spanish class last year. How did you know?" Bella asked.

"Rosa's teaching me Spanish so I can talk better to my friend Carlos."

Carrie beamed at them and gave Wyatt a significant look. Yeah. She was definitely matchmaking, despite the way he had basically told her to stand down the last time.

He was going to have to do whatever he could to deflect any of Carrie's efforts in that department.

To his relief, his sister was not overtly obvious over dinner, though she did suggest he and Rosa take a look at how her climbing roses were growing, something they both managed to avoid by changing the subject.

Having his sister and her family there, along with Logan, helped make things a little less awkward between them, but he still couldn't help remembering his hurt when she had told him they should avoid being together.

The food was good, at least. Carrie had a great marinade he always enjoyed and Joe was a whiz at the grill. Really, any time Wyatt didn't have to cook, he was happy.

Rosa was too busy talking to Bella and Logan to seem bothered by his presence.

After they ate, Rosa was the first to stand up. "Thank you for dinner, but things were so chaotic as I was leaving work that I am afraid I was not thinking. I just remembered I left some invoices I need to pay tonight on my desk. I would not want to leave them there overnight. Will you excuse me?"

Carrie made a face. "You're not staying for dessert? It's homemade vanilla ice cream that Bella helped me make this afternoon."

Rosa gave a vague smile. "It sounds very good but I really do need to go. Thank you, though."

She hugged both females and Logan, then waved to Wyatt and Joe before hurrying away.

After she left, some of the sparkle seemed to go out of the evening. Wyatt knew he wasn't the only one who felt it.

She was definitely trying to avoid him. He could only hope that everyone else didn't guess that her reasons for leaving so abruptly had anything to do with him.

"I'll have ice cream," Logan said.

"Same here," Bella said. "It's delicious."

He had to agree. It *was* delicious. But all that frozen, creamy sweetness still couldn't remove the sour taste in his mouth.

"Dinner was great," he said after everyone had finished dessert. "Logan, let's help with dishes."

His son groaned a little but stood up to help clear away plates and carry them back inside the house.

When the dishwasher was loaded, Bella asked if she and Logan could take Hank for a walk before Wyatt left with the dog for home. He almost said no but was in no hurry to return to the tension of Brambleberry House.

"Sure. I can wait a little longer."

Logan was staying the night again with his aunt and uncle because Wyatt had an early meeting.

Joe got a phone call from his parents, who lived in Arizona, and excused himself to talk to them for a few moments, leaving Wyatt alone with Carrie.

"How's the house coming?" Carrie asked after her husband left the room.

"Almost there, I'm happy to report. We should be able to move back in another few weeks."

"That seems fast. But living at Brambleberry House worked out well, didn't it?"

A week ago, he would have said yes. "It's been fine. Logan has enjoyed having his own room again. It's a lovely old house and our apartment is roomier than our actual house."

"I'm glad. And your neighbors are nice, both of them. I like Jen and Rosa."

That was another area of frustration. He hadn't been able to make much progress in Jen's situation, other than to alert the department and do a little online sleuthing. Aaron Barker seemed to be a good cop, from what he could find out. He had no black marks on his reputation that Wyatt could find after a cursory search.

At least nothing suspicious seemed to have happened since Jen had told him about her stalker. He had been extra vigilant but hadn't learned anything new.

"Rosa is lovely, isn't she?" Carrie said in a casual voice that did not fool him for an instant.

He finally voiced the suspicion that had been nagging at him since he discovered Rosa had also been invited to dinner.

"I don't suppose there's any chance you're trying to push Rosa and me together, even after I told you not to, is there?"

"Me? Would I do that? Don't be silly." She gave him a shocked sort of look but he knew his sister well enough to see past it easily. She would do that kind of thing in a heartbeat, if she thought he might have the slightest interest in Rosa.

"Are you sure? This is the second time you've invited us both to dinner. Come to think of it, you seemed pretty determined that I move into her empty apartment at Brambleberry House."

"Only because it was the perfect solution when you yourself talked about moving out! I was only trying to help. As for dinner, it just so happens she is my dear friend and you are my brother. I like spending time visiting with each of you. I can't help it if sometimes those visits overlap."

"Can't you?"

"I didn't realize it would be a problem," she said rather stiffly. "I thought you and Rosa were friends. Logan is always talking about how she's teaching him Spanish and how much he loves her dog and how you go out for tacos together."

He frowned. "That was one time, when we bumped into each other at the taco stand. Rosa and I are friends. That's all. Neither one of us is in the market for a relationship right now. I told you that."

"But you two are perfect for each other!"

Wyatt felt that little tug on his heart again, remembering how Rosa had held him during his moment of despair over the ugly crime scene he had just left, generously offering him a comfort and peace he had desperately needed.

He was beginning to think Carrie was right, at least on one side of the equation. Rosa was perfect for him. Smart, sweet, kind. He loved how warm she was with Logan and how compassionate and protective she was for her friend.

None of that mattered. Not when she had made it clear she wanted nothing to do with him except friendship.

"It's not going to happen. Get it out of your head, please. I would hate for you to make things awkward between us."

Carrie looked deeply disappointed. "It's just that I love her, you know? I want her to be happy. I want *you* to be happy. Why shouldn't you be happy together? I guess I just thought…after everything she's been through, she deserved a wonderful guy like you."

He frowned. "That's the second time you've made reference to something in her past. What do you know? What has she been through?"

Carrie immediately looked away, but not before he saw guilt flash in her eyes. "Life can be hard for people trying to make it in a new country. She came here with nothing. She didn't even speak the language well. How fortunate she was to find her adoptive family, Anna Galvez's brother and his wife."

There was something else here. Something he couldn't quite put his finger on. A suspicion had begun to take root but it was one he didn't even dare ask his sister.

What if he was wrong?

Meantime, he had to do what he could to divert Carrie's attention and prevent her from meddling further between the two of them.

"Rosa is an extraordinary woman. I agree. But I'm not looking for anybody, no matter how extraordinary. Got that?"

She looked as if she wanted to argue, but to his relief, she finally sighed. "Fine. I won't invite you both to dinner, unless it's a party that includes a bunch of other people."

Would he be able to handle even that much? Right now, he wasn't sure. At least he would be moving away from Brambleberry House within the next few weeks. When he wasn't living downstairs from her, perhaps he could stop dreaming about her and wishing he could hold her again.

Chapter Thirteen

It was fully dark when Rosa returned to Bramble-berry House after stopping at By-The-Wind and running the bills to the post-office drop box.

She hadn't been lying about the invoices. She really had forgotten them, though mailing them certainly could have waited until the next day. That had been sheer fiction, an excuse to escape the tension between her and Wyatt.

She always loved spending time with the Abbotts. Carrie was invariably warm and kind and Joe treated her like a beloved younger sister.

And then there was Bella, full of energy and fun and enthusiasm for life. Her mood always seemed to rub off on Rosa, leaving her happier than when she had arrived.

This time, though, Rosa couldn't shake a deep sense of melancholy.

She knew the reason. Because Wyatt and Logan had been there. Spending time with them was beginning to make her ache deep inside.

She knew she was setting herself up for heartbreak. She could sense it hovering, just out of sight.

She was falling for them. Both of them.

Logan was impossible to resist. His sweet personality and eagerness to learn touched something deep inside of her. She would be so sad when he was no longer a regular part of her life.

And Wyatt. She brushed a lock of hair from her eyes. It was very possible that Wyatt was the most wonderful man she had ever met. She wanted to wrap her arms around him and not let go.

She could not, though. Rosa knew she could not have what she wanted.

She knew people who spent their entire lives wanting something other than what they had. Rosa tried not to be that person.

As a girl growing up with little in the way of material things, she had become used to that feeling of lack. Mostly, she had learned to ignore it, instead finding happiness with what she *did* have.

She was part owner in a business she loved running, she lived in a beautiful house at the seaside, she had cherished friends and a loving family. Most of the time, those things were enough.

Once in a while, though, like on moonlit summer nights, she caught glimpses of the future she might have had if not for a few foolish choices, and it made her heart ache.

Rosa sighed, a sad sound that seemed to echo in the emptiness of her apartment. Fiona nudged at her leg, resting her chin on Rosa's knee and gazing at her out of eyes that seemed filled with empathy.

Sometimes the dog seemed to sense her emotions keenly and offered exactly the right thing to lift her mood.

"You want to go for a walk, don't you?"

Fiona wagged her tail wildly in agreement. Rosa sighed again. She had let her dog out when she first came home a short time earlier, but apparently that was not enough for her, especially when the work day had been so hectic and she hadn't had time to take her on a walk.

Rosa was tired and not really in the mood for a nighttime walk. Part of being a responsible pet owner, though, was doing what she didn't always feel like doing when it was in the best interest of her beloved Fi.

"Okay. Let's find your leash."

Fiona scampered to the hook by the door of the apartment, where Rosa kept all the tools necessary for a walk. A hoodie, Fi's leash, a flashlight, treats and waste bags.

A few moments later, she headed down the steps. They had just reached the bottom when the door to Wyatt's apartment suddenly opened.

She gave a little gasp of surprise when he and Hank came out, the cute little dog all but straining on the leash.

"Oh," Rosa exclaimed. "You startled me."

Wyatt made a face. "Sorry. Hank was in a mood and nothing seemed to be settling him down. I was just going to take him on a quick walk. Are you coming or going?"

"Going. Fiona was in the same mood as Hank."

"Maybe they're talking to each other through the pipes."

Despite her lingering melancholy, Rosa had to smile a little at that idea. Fiona was smart enough that she could probably figure out a way to communicate to other dogs inside the house.

She looked behind him. "Where is Logan?"

"He's sleeping over at Carrie's again. I've got an early meeting tomorrow so they offered to keep him after dinner so I don't have to drag him out of bed so early."

"That is nice of them. Your sister is very kind."

"Truth. She is the best. I would have been lost without her after Tori died. Totally lost. She and

Joe have been amazing, basically stepping in to help me parent Logan."

The dogs seemed delighted to see each other, sniffing like crazy with their tails wagging a hundred miles an hour.

She knew it was impossible, but Rosa still could not shake the suspicion that somehow her dog had manipulated events exactly this way, so that she and Wyatt would meet in the entryway of the house.

He opened the door and they both walked out into the evening, lit by a full moon that made her flashlight superfluous.

"Want to walk together?" he asked after a moment.

His suggestion surprised her so much that she did not know how to answer for a moment. Intellectually, she knew she was supposed to be maintaining a careful distance between them. She did not want to fall any harder for him.

How could she say no, though? Especially when she knew her time with him was so fleeting?

"That makes sense, doesn't it?"

"Which direction were you going? To the beach?"

Usually she liked to stick to the paths with streetlights and some traffic when she was walking late at night. Since Wyatt was with her, that wasn't necessary.

"Yes. Let's walk on the beach. The water always calls me."

They walked through the gardens, the air sweet with the scent of flowers and herbs. He opened the gate for her and she and Fiona went first down the path to the sand.

The moon was bright and full, casting a pearly blue light on everything. She certainly did not need her flashlight.

They walked mostly in silence for the first few moments, content to let the sounds of the waves fill the void. Despite everything between them, it was a comfortable silence.

She was the first to break it. "You said at dinner that your house is almost finished. Is everything going the way you like?"

"Yes. We had a few issues early on. It's an old house with electrical issues, which is what started the fire in the first place. I want to make sure everything is exactly right. I think I have been getting on the electrician's nerves a little, but we're getting there."

He gave her a sidelong look. "I'm sure you'll be glad when everything is finished so we can get out of your way."

"You are not in my way," she protested. It wasn't exactly the truth. He was very much in the way of her thoughts constantly. "You know you can stay as long as you need."

"I know. Thank you for that."

"I am sure you are more than ready to be back in your house."

He shrugged. "I suppose."

"You do not sound convinced."

"It's just a house, you know? I bought it after Tori died, when I knew I needed help and the best thing would be to move near Carrie and Joe. That one was available and it was close but it's never really felt like a home."

She had not been to his house and couldn't offer an opinion, but she had to wonder if the house needed a woman's touch.

She did not want to think about any other woman going in and decorating his house with warm, comfortable touches. She wanted to be the one turning his house into a home.

She pushed away the thought.

"You had many changes in a short time. That can be hard for anyone."

"I guess."

They walked in silence for a few more moments, stopping only when Hank lifted his leg against a tuft of grass.

"Carrie said something tonight that made me curious." He spoke slowly, as if choosing his words with care.

"Oh?"

"Something about you. She implied you had a

tough time after you came to the United States. It made me wonder again how you came to be adopted after you arrived. That seems unusual. You were a teenager, right?"

Rosa tensed, remembering that horrible time in her life, full of fear and darkness and things she did not like to think about.

"Yes. Fifteen."

"And you didn't have family here or back in Honduras who could have helped you?"

Her heart seemed to squeeze at the memory of her dear mother, who had tried so hard to give Rosa a better life. She gripped Fiona's leash. The dog, who had been cavorting with Hank, suddenly returned to her side as if sensing Rosa's distress.

"No."

"How did you get here?"

That was a long and twisted story.

"I told you my mother died. I had no money and no family. A friend of my mother's told me I could find work at a factory in the city. She helped me find a place to live with some other girls and gave me a little money."

"That's nice."

"Yes. But then some men came to the factory telling us they knew of many jobs we could do across the border. I was afraid and didn't want to, but other girls, my friends, said yes. Then I...had some trouble with my boss at the factory and he fired me."

She thought of how innocent she had been in those days. Her mother had tried to shelter her when she was alive. As a result, Rosa knew little about the world or how to protect herself from men who wanted to take advantage of her. First her boss, then those offering riches and jobs in a new world. She had been monumentally naive, had thought maybe she would be working in another factory in the United States, one that paid better.

She had been so very wrong.

She was not going to tell any of that to Wyatt.

"What did you do then?"

"I came here and shortly after, I met Daniel and Lauren and they took me in and helped me go to school and then become a citizen," she said quickly.

He gave her a searching look through the darkness, as if he knew full well there had to be more to her story. She lifted her chin and continued walking, pretending that Fiona had led her a little ahead of him and Hank.

She didn't want him to press her about this. If he did, she would have to turn around and go back to the house without him. To her relief, he seemed to know she had told him all she was going to about that time.

"They must be very kind people."

She seized gratefully on his words. "The best. I told you Daniel is a sheriff in Utah and Lauren is a doctor. I was very lucky they found me."

She knew it was more than luck. It was a miracle. She had prayed to the Virgin and to her own mother that someone would help her, that she could find some light in the darkness. And then, literally, a light had found her hiding in the back of a pickup truck in the middle of a January storm. She had been beaten and bloodied, and had been semiconscious when Daniel and Lauren had found her. They had pulled her from that pickup truck and had saved her. An answer to her prayers.

They had stood by her then as she had spoken out against those who had hurt her. And they had stood by her later when she had to make the most difficult decision of her life.

"Carrie talked about how much courage it must have taken you to make your way in a new country."

Rosa loved her country and her people. People from Honduras called themselves and each other *Catrachos*, a name that had come to mean resilience and solidarity.

She would always consider herself part *Catracha* but this was her home now.

If her mother had not died, she might have stayed and built a happy life there. She probably would have married young and would have had several children by now.

After Daniel and Lauren rescued her, she had been able to get an education that would have been completely out of reach to her in that small, poor village.

"Courage? No. I had nothing there after my mother died. And here I had a family. People who loved me and wanted the best for me. That was everything to me. It still is."

Wyatt could not doubt the quiet sincerity in her voice. She loved the people who had taken her in.

He was suddenly deeply grateful for them, too. He would have loved the chance to have met them in person to tell them so.

They walked in silence for a few more moments, heading back toward Brambleberry House, which stood like a beacon above the beach a short distance away.

He could tell Rosa did not like talking about this. Her body language conveyed tension. He should let it go now. Her secrets were none of his business, but since she had told him this much, perhaps she would trust him and tell him the rest of it.

"You said you were fifteen when you came here?"

"Yes," she said, her voice clipped.

How had she even made it across several borders? And what about the men who had promised her work in the United States?

He wasn't stupid. He could guess what kind of work they wanted from her and it made him sick to his stomach. Sex trafficking was a huge problem, especially among young girls smuggled in from other countries.

Was that what Daniel and Lauren had rescued her from?

He couldn't seem to find the words to ask. Or to ask her how she had escaped. He was quite sure he would not like the answer.

How was it possible? She was the most loving and giving person he knew, kind to everyone. How could she have emerged from something so ugly to become the person he was falling for?

Maybe he was wrong. He truly hoped he was wrong.

"You could have found yourself in all kinds of danger at that young age."

"Yes."

She said nothing more, only looked ahead at her dog and at the house, now only a hundred feet away.

He thought again of his suspicions earlier that evening at dinner. He was beginning to think they might not be far-fetched, after all.

"I think my sister is right," he said quietly when

they reached the beach gate to the house. "You are a remarkable person, Rosa Galvez."

Her face was a blur in the moonlight as she gazed at him, her eyes dark shadows. She shook her head. "I am not. Lauren and Daniel, who reached out to me when I was afraid and vulnerable, they are the remarkable ones."

Tenderness swirled through him. She was amazing and he was falling hard for her. Learning more details about what she had endured and overcome, including the things she hadn't yet shared with him, only intensified his growing feelings.

"We will have to agree to disagree on that one," he finally said. "Every time I'm with you, I find something else to admire."

"Don't," she said sharply. "You don't know."

"I know I think about you all the time. I can't seem to stop."

"You shouldn't."

"I know that. Believe me, I know. But you're in my head now."

And in my heart, he thought, but wasn't quite ready to share that with her yet.

"May I kiss you again?"

Because of what he suspected had happened to her, it became more important than ever to ask permission first and not just take what he wanted.

He thought she would refuse at first, that she

would turn into the house. After a long moment, she lifted her face to his.

"Yes," she murmured, almost as if she couldn't help herself.

This kiss was tender, gentle, a mere brush of his mouth against hers.

All the feelings he had been fighting seemed to shimmer to the surface. He could tell himself all he wanted that he was not ready to care for someone again. He could tell everyone else the same story. That did not make it true.

He had already fallen. Somehow Rosa Galvez, with her kindness and her empathy and her determination to do the right thing, had reached into the bleak darkness where he had been existing and ripped away the heavy curtains to let sunshine flood in again.

He was not sure yet how he felt about that. Some part of him wanted to stay frozen in his sadness. He had loved Tori with all his heart. Their marriage had not been perfect—he wasn't sure any healthy marriage could be completely without differences—but she had been a great mother and a wonderful wife.

Wyatt wasn't sure he was ready to risk his heart again.

But maybe he didn't have a choice. Maybe he had already fallen.

He wrapped his arms around her tightly, wanting to protect her from all the darkness in the world. She made a small sound and nestled against him, as if searching for warmth and safety.

"I lied to my sister," he said, long moments later.

He felt her smile against his mouth. "For shame, Detective Townsend. How did you lie to Carrie?"

He brushed a strand of hair away from her face. "She admitted after you left that she invited us both to dinner because she has some wild idea of matchmaking."

Instead of continuing to smile, as he thought she would, Rosa suddenly looked distressed.

Her eyes widened and her hands slipped away from around his neck. "Oh, no."

He nodded. "I told her to get that idea out of her head. I told her we were only friends and would never be anything more than that."

She stepped away. "You told her the truth. That is not a lie. We *are* friends."

"But we're more than that, aren't we?"

She folded her hands together, her mouth trembling a little. "No. What you said to her is the truth. We are friends. Only that."

"You can really say that after that kiss?"

"Sharing a few kisses does not make us lovers, Wyatt. Surely you see this."

He wasn't sure why she was so upset but she was all but wringing her hands.

"This thing between us is not exactly your average friendship, either. You have to admit that. I have lots of friends and I don't stay up nights thinking about kissing them."

She made a small, upset sound and reached for her dog's leash.

"We cannot do this anymore, Wyatt. You must see that. I was wrong to let you kiss me. To—to kiss you back. I should have stopped you."

She started moving toward the house. He gazed after her, hurt at her abrupt dismissal of what had felt like an emotional, beautiful moment between them.

He knew she had felt it, as well. Rosa was not the sort of woman who would kiss someone with so much sweetness and eagerness without at least some feeling behind it.

He quickly caught up with her just as she pushed open the beach gate and walked into the Brambleberry House gardens.

"Why are you so determined to push me away? What aren't you telling me?"

"Nothing. I told you before—I am not looking for this in my life right now."

"I wasn't, either, but I think it's found us. I care about you, Rosa. Very much. For the first time since Tori died, I want to spend time with a woman. And I might be crazy but I suspect you wouldn't kiss me if you didn't have similar feelings for me. Am I wrong?"

She was silent for a moment. When she faced him, her chin was up again and her eyes seemed without expression.

"Yes. You are wrong," she said, her voice muted. "I do not have feelings for you. It is impossible. You are the brother of my friend and you are my tenant who will be leaving soon. That is all you are to me, Wyatt. I… You must not kiss me again. Ever. Do you understand this? No matter what, you must not."

She turned and hurried for the house, leaving him staring after her, hurt and confusion and rejection tumbling through him.

She sounded so very certain that he could not question her conviction. Apparently he had misunderstood everything. All this time, he had been falling for her, but the feeling apparently was not mutual.

She had told him they should stay away from each other. Why had he not listened?

He knew the answer to that. His feelings were growing so strong that he couldn't believe they could possibly be one-sided.

Lord, he was an idiot. No different than Jenna's cop, who couldn't accept rejection even after it slapped him in the face.

He should have kept his mouth shut. She had told him over and over that she was not interested in a relationship with him, but he'd been too stubborn to listen.

Now he just had to figure out how he was going to go on without her.

Rosa sat in her darkened apartment a short time later, window open to the ocean and Fiona at her feet. Usually she found solace in the sound of the waves but not now.

This night, it seemed to echo through Brambleberry House, accentuating how very alone she felt.

What had she done? With all her heart, she wished she could go downstairs, knock on his door and tell Wyatt *she* was the one lying now.

I do not have feelings for you. It is impossible. You are the brother of my friend and you are my tenant who will be leaving soon. That is all you are to me, Wyatt.

None of those words were true, of course. Or at least not the whole truth. She cared about Wyatt, more than any man she had ever known. She was falling in love with him. Here in the quiet solitude of her apartment, she could admit the truth.

She realized now that she had started to fall for him the first time she met Carrie's brother with the sad eyes and the adorable little boy.

How could she not love him? He was everything good and kind she admired in a man. He was a loving father, a loyal brother, a dedicated detective. An honorable man.

That was the very reason she had no choice but to push him away. Wyatt deserved a woman with no demons. Someone courageous and good.

If he knew the truth about her and her choices, he would quickly see how wrong he was about her.

The walls of the house did not embrace her with comfort, as they usually did.

Somehow, it felt cold and even sad. For some ridiculous reason, Rosa felt as if she had faced some sort of test and she had failed spectacularly.

It was a silly feeling, she knew. Houses could not be sad.

Fiona lifted her head suddenly and gazed off at nothing, then whimpered for no reason. Rosa frowned. There was no such thing as ghosts, either. And absolutely no reason for her to feel guilty, as if she had failed Abigail somehow.

"I had to push him away," she said aloud, though she wasn't sure just who she was trying to convince. Fiona, Abigail or herself. "Someday he will see that I was right. He will be glad I at least could see that we cannot be together."

Fiona huffed out a breath while Abigail said nothing, of course.

As for Rosa, her heart felt as if it was going to crack apart. She knew it would not. She had been through hard things before—she would figure out a way to survive this.

In a short time, he and his son would be moving out of Brambleberry House and back to their own home. As before, she would only see them occasionally. Maybe on the street, maybe at some town celebration. Maybe even at a party with Joe and Carrie. She could be polite and even friendly.

Wyatt did not ever need to know about these cracks in her heart, or how hard she found it to think about moving forward with her life without him, and without Logan.

Chapter Fourteen

Somehow, she wasn't sure exactly how, Rosa made it through most of the next week without seeing either Logan or Wyatt.

They seemed to leave early in the morning and come back late at night. She could only guess they were hard at work on the part of renovations Wyatt was handling on their house and getting it ready for their move back.

This guess was confirmed when she came home for lunch one day and found a note tucked into her door.

Repairs to the house are done, the note said in bold, scrawling handwriting. *We will be moving out tomorrow. Wyatt.*

Rosa had to catch her breath as pain sliced through her at the brusque, clipped note and at the message it contained.

Tomorrow. A week earlier than he had planned. He must have spent every available moment trying to finish things in his eagerness to get out of her house and her life.

She returned to the store with a heavy heart but a sense of relief, as well. She could not begin to put back together the pieces of her life when he was living two floors below her.

Even when she did not see him or Logan, she was still constantly aware they were both so close and yet completely out of her reach.

When she walked into the store, she found Jen laughing at something with a customer. The change in her friend was remarkable. She looked bright and pretty and happy, a far cry from the withdrawn, frightened woman she had been when she first came to Cannon Beach.

Jen finished ringing up the customer with a genuine smile Rosa once had feared she would not see again.

"You are in a good mood," she said.

"Yes. I heard from the online graduate program I've been in touch with. I've been accepted for fall semester and they're offering a financial-aid package that will cover almost the whole tuition."

"That's terrific! Oh, Jen. I'm so happy for you.

How will you juggle teaching, graduate school and Addie at the same time?"

"It's going to be tricky but I think I can handle it, especially now that she's starting first grade. I can do the coursework at night after she's in bed. It will take me a few years, but when I'm done, it will open up other career doors for me."

"Oh, I am so happy for you."

Jen beamed at her. "It's all because of you. I never would have had the courage to even apply if you hadn't been in my corner, pushing me out of my comfort zone."

Rosa might not have a happily-ever-after with the man she was falling in love with. But she had good friends and wanted to think she was making a difference in their lives, a little bit at a time.

"We should celebrate tonight," Rosa said.

"You don't have a hot date?"

She made a face. "Not me. I have no date, hot or otherwise."

"What about our sexy neighbor?" Jen teased.

That terse note of his flashed through her mind again and her chest gave a sharp spasm.

"He will not be our neighbor long. Wyatt and Logan are moving out in the morning."

Jen's smile slid away. "Oh, no! Addie will miss having them around. She has really enjoyed playing with Logan in the evenings. I thought they wouldn't be moving for a few more weeks."

"Apparently, their house is finished. Wyatt left me a note on the door when I went home for lunch and to bring back Fiona."

Jen gave her a sharp look that Rosa pretended not to see.

"My evening is totally free," she said, "and I would love nothing more than to celebrate with you. Do you want to go somewhere?"

Jen gazed out the window. "It looks like it's going to be another beautiful night. I would be just as happy taking Fiona for a walk on the beach and then grabbing dinner at the taco truck. I think Addie would be all over that, too."

Rosa was not sure she would ever be able to eat at the taco truck without remembering that delightful evening with Logan and Wyatt, but for the sake of her friend, she would do her best.

"Done."

The store was busy with customers the rest of the afternoon. Rosa preferred it that way. Having something to do gave her less time to think.

Jen's shift was supposed to end at five, but during a lull in the hectic pace about a half hour before that, Rosa pulled her aside. "Your shift is almost over and Paula and Juan will be here soon for the evening shift. Why don't you go pick up Addie from her day care and I will meet you at home?"

"Sounds great."

Jen took off her apron, then hung it on the hook in the back room and quickly left.

Rosa was going to miss having her around when school started, not just because she was a good worker, but Rosa enjoyed her company. They made a good team.

She finished ringing up two more customers, then spent a few more moments talking to the married older couple who helped her out a few nights a week during busy summer months.

Finally, she and Fiona walked out into a lovely July evening. The dog was eager for a walk and Rosa was, too. She was looking forward to the evening with Addie and Jen. Tacos and good friends. What was not to enjoy?

When she neared the house, she didn't see Wyatt's SUV. Rosa told herself she was glad.

Perhaps she wouldn't have to see him at all before he moved out the next day.

Fiona went immediately to the backyard. When Rosa followed her, she found Jen and Addie on the tree swing. Addie's legs were stretched out as she tried to pump and she looked so filled with joy, Rosa had to smile.

"Look at me!" Addie called. "I'm flying!"

"You are doing so well at swinging," Rosa exclaimed.

"I know. I never went so high before."

She almost told her to be careful but caught

herself. She wanted all little girls to soar as high as they dared.

"We got home about a half hour ago and haven't even been inside yet," Jen said with a laugh. "Addie insisted she had to swing first."

"It is very fun," Rosa agreed. Addie's excitement and Jen's good mood went a long way to cheering her up.

She might not have everything she wanted but her life could still be rich and beautiful. She had to remember that.

"I noticed the handsome detective isn't home yet. I was going to see if he wanted to come with us to the taco truck."

Jen spoke so casually that Rosa almost missed the mischievous look in her eyes.

Rosa avoided her gaze. "He is probably at his house making sure things are ready for him and Logan to return home tomorrow."

"I'll miss them."

Rosa wasn't sure she liked that pensive note in her friend's voice. Was Jen interested in Wyatt, as well?

Why wouldn't she be? He was a wonderful man and Jen was exactly the sort of woman who could make him happy. The two of them would be very good together, even though the idea of it made Rosa's chest hurt.

"When you are ready to date again, maybe you

should think about dating Wyatt. You both have a lot in common."

Jen gave her a shocked, rather appalled look that Rosa thought was out of proportion to her mild suggestion. "Besides being single parents, I don't think so."

"He's a widower, you're a widow," she pointed out.

"True. And that's the only thing we have in common. Don't get me wrong. I like Wyatt a lot. He seems very nice. But I don't think he would be interested in me. His interests appear to lie... elsewhere."

Jen gave her such a significant look that Rosa could feel her face heat.

I care about you, Rosa. Very much. For the first time since Tori died, I want to spend time with a woman. And I might be crazy but I suspect you wouldn't kiss me if you didn't have similar feelings for me.

Wyatt would soon forget her and any wild idea he had that he might have feelings for her.

Before she could answer, she heard a noise and saw someone walk around the side of the house to where they were.

For a moment, with the setting sun shining on his face, she thought it might be Wyatt. Her heart skipped a beat and she felt foolish, hoping he hadn't heard their conversation.

Jen suddenly gasped, her features going instantly pale, and Rosa realized her mistake.

This was not Wyatt. It was a man she didn't recognize.

This man was big, solid, with wide shoulders and a rather thick neck. He had close-cropped brown hair and blue eyes that should have been attractive but were somehow cold.

Fiona, at her feet, instantly rose and growled a little, moving protectively in front of the two of them. That didn't seem to stop the man, who continued walking until he was only a few feet away.

"Jenna," he said, gazing at her friend with an odd, intense, almost possessive look. "Here you are. It is you. It took me forever to track you down."

Rosa knew instantly who this was. Who else could it be? Aaron Barker, the police officer who was stalking Jen and had driven her from her Utah home to Cannon Beach. She should have realized it the moment the color leached away from Jen's features.

Jenna stood frozen for a moment as if she couldn't remember how to move, then she quickly moved to the side and stopped the swing, pulling Addie off and into her arms.

"Hey!" the girl exclaimed. "I'm not done swinging."

Addie started to complain but something of her mother's tension seemed to trickle to the girl. She fell silent, eying the adults around her with sudden wariness.

"What do you want?" Jen asked. Her voice shook slightly.

"I've missed you so much, baby. Aren't you happy to see me?" He took another step forward as if to embrace her. Jen quickly stepped back.

Rosa didn't know what to do. They were on the side of the house without an entrance. The only way to get inside to safety was through the front door. To get there, they would have to go around this man.

Aaron Barker was dangerous. She recognized the fierce, violent look in his eyes. She had seen that before...

Old, long-suppressed panic started to bubble up inside her, those demons she thought she had vanquished long ago.

Rosa drew in a harsh breath and then another, suddenly desperate to escape.

No. She had to protect her friend. She wouldn't let her be hurt again.

"What do you want?" Jen asked again. She took a sideways step, Addie in her arms, and Rosa realized she was edging closer to the front door.

"Just to talk. That's all."

Jenna shuffled to the side another step and Rosa moved, as well, hoping he hadn't noticed.

"I don't want to talk to you. I tried that before and you wouldn't listen. Please. Just leave me alone."

He moved as if to come closer but Fiona growled. She wasn't particularly fierce-looking with her long, soft fur and her sweet eyes, but she did have sharp teeth.

The dog's show of courage gave Rosa strength to draw upon her own.

"You heard her."

Jen took another sideways step and Rosa did, too. The front porch was still so very far away.

"This is private property," she went on. "You are trespassing. Please leave."

"I'm not leaving without talking to Jenna." When he spoke, she caught a definite whiff of alcohol on his breath. He had been drinking and he already had to be unstable to put Jenna through long months of torture. Rosa knew this was not a good combination.

"She clearly does not want to talk to you."

"She has to."

"No. She does not." Hoping to distract him further from realizing she and Jenna had maneuvered so that they were now closer to the door than he was, Rosa reached into her pocket for her cell phone. "I must ask you again to leave or I will have to call nine-one-one."

"You think that worries me? I'm a police officer."

"Not here," she said firmly. "The police here do not stand by while someone hurts a woman, even if he is also a police officer."

She had to hope that was true of all officers in the Cannon Beach Police Department and not only Wyatt.

"Now. I am asking you for the final time to leave or I will call the police."

Now Jenna was backing toward the door and Rosa did the same, with Fiona still standing protectively in front of them.

He frowned. "I'm not leaving without Jenna. We love each other."

He took another step closer and from behind Rosa, Jen made a small sound of panic.

"Jenna. Go inside. Call nine-one-one."

She must have made a move toward the house because several things happened at once. Aaron Barker growled out a sound of frustration and lunged for her. Fiona jumped into protective mode and latched on to his leg and he kicked out at the dog, who whimpered and fell to the ground.

"No! Fi!" Rosa cried out. The coward pulled his leg back as if to kick again and Rosa instantly dropped to the ground, her body over the dog's.

Seconds later, she felt crushing pain in her back and realized he had kicked *her* instead of the dog.

This was the first time in fifteen years someone had struck out at her in anger. Instantly, she was transported to another time, another place. The past broke free of the prison where she kept it, the memories pouring over her like acid.

Other boots. Other fists. Again and again until she was in agony as vicious words in Spanish called her horrible names and told her she was going to die.

Something whimpered beneath her and the past suddenly receded—she was back in the present with her back throbbing and her dog wriggling beneath her.

Fiona was alive, and was just winded like Rosa. Thank God.

She could not just lie here trying to catch her breath. She had to protect her friend. Already, the man was making his way past Rosa and the dog toward the porch, where Jenna was desperately trying to punch in the code to unlock the door.

"I'm sorry, baby," Rosa said to Fi, then rose shakily to her feet. Her amazing dog was right behind her and she realized Fi had been whimpering for her to get up so they could both keep fighting.

Rosa ignored her pain as she limped after him.

"Stop. Right now," she said. He had almost reached the porch and Rosa did the only thing she could think of to slow him down. Though her back groaned with pain, she jumped on him, her arms around his neck as she had been taught in the self-defense classes Daniel had insisted she take.

He cried out in frustration and swung his elbows back, trying to get her off. One elbow caught her mouth and she tasted blood but still she clung tightly.

"Stupid dog!" he cried out again and she realized Fiona must have bitten him again to protect them.

She was so busy hanging on for dear life, she almost missed the sound of the door opening as Jenna finally managed to unlock it. She could see the other woman looked undecided whether to go inside to safety or come to Rosa's aid.

"Go," she yelled to Jenna. "Call nine-one-one."

An instant later, she heard the sound of the dead bolt. She was so relieved, she relaxed her hold slightly, but it was enough for him to shake her off as Fiona would with a sand fly.

She fell to the grass, barely missing the walkway, and rolled out of the way of his kicking boots. Fiona was still growling but had retreated also, and now came to stand in front of her.

"You bitch," he growled. "You stupid bitch. This is none of your damn business."

She could hardly breathe, but she managed to squeeze out a few words. "My friend. My house. My business."

He started for the door and she grabbed the closest weapon she could find, a rock from the flower garden. Rosa stood up and held it tightly.

"I will not let you hurt her," she gasped out.

He appeared genuinely shocked by that. "I would never hurt Jenna. Never. I love her and she loves me."

He ran a hand through his hair. The man was definitely unhinged, whether from his obsession or from alcohol, she did not know. What did it matter? She only knew there was no point in arguing with him. She longed for the safety of the house, but didn't know how she could get inside without him following her and having access to Jenna.

"How can you say you love her? She ran away from you."

"I've been out of my head, worried about her. She disappeared in the middle of the night and no one would tell me where she went."

He sounded so plaintive that she would have felt sorry for him if she didn't know the torture he had put Jenna through these past few months.

"How did you...find her?" She was so afraid and in pain, she could barely breathe enough to get the question out, but had some wild thought that if she could keep him talking, perhaps the police would arrive before he killed her.

"Luck," he growled. "Sheer luck. A friend who knew how broke up I was about her leaving said he thought he saw someone who looked like her working in a gift shop when he was here on vacation with his family."

Rosa closed her eyes, remembering that day Jen had thought she saw someone she recognized. She had been right. Completely right.

"How did you know it was Jenna?"

He shrugged. "I'm a cop. I've got connections. I traced her Social Security number and found an employment record here at some shop in town. I figured they wouldn't tell me where she lived so I asked at the shop next door."

All their efforts to protect her hadn't been enough. Rosa had never thought of putting their neighboring stores on alert. She felt stupid for not thinking of it.

"As soon as I heard she might be here, I had to see if it was her." His face darkened. "I have to talk to her. Make sure she's okay."

"You have seen her. Jenna is fine. She wants you now to leave her alone."

"I'm not going to do that. We love each other. She's just being stubborn."

Rosa stood in front of him on the porch, Fiona growling at her side. "You cannot see her now."

She could see his talkative mood shift to anger again.

"Get out of my way," he said slowly and deliberately, and moved a step closer.

"No," she said, gripping the rock more tightly.

"You think I'm going to let some stupid little

bitch keep me away from the woman I love after I've come all this way?"

Always, it was about him. Not about the woman or the child he had displaced from their home, forced to flee his unwanted obsession.

Rosa was shaking and she realized it was a combination of fear, pain and anger.

"Get out of my way. If you think I'm leaving, you don't know a damn thing about me."

Rosa lifted her chin. "I know all I need to know about you, Aaron Barker. I know you are a coward, a bully, a despicable human being. You have terrorized Jenna, one of the kindest women I know, who has already been through enough, because you refuse to believe a woman is not interested in you."

"Shut up. Jenna loves me."

"Then why did she move eight hundred miles to get away from you?"

His face turned red with anger. "Move. Last warning."

"I am not going anywhere."

He reached to shove her aside and Fiona lunged again. He kicked out at the dog, but she would not let her sweet canine protector be hurt again.

Rosa lifted the rock with both hands and, with every ounce of strength she had left, she slammed it into the side of his head. He stared at her in shock, dazed, then staggered backward, stumbling off the porch.

Rosa stared at him for only a second before she rushed to the door. She was fumbling to punch in the code when she heard sirens and a door slam, then a voice yelled out, "Don't move!"

Wyatt!

He had come.

Vast relief poured over her and Rosa, shaking violently now, sagged to the ground, her back pressed against the door and her arms wrapped around her brave, wonderful dog.

Chapter Fifteen

Wyatt restrained the son of a bitch, who seemed groggy and incoherent, and was mumbling about how much he loved Jen and how she had to talk to him.

It took every ounce of control he had not to bash the man's head against the porch steps, especially when he saw blood trickling out of Rosa's mouth.

This man had hurt Rosa. And not just physically. She looked...shattered. He wanted to go to her, but he needed to secure the scene first before he could comfort her.

"Where are Jen and Addie?" he asked. He had been at his sister's house when Jen had called, her voice frantic. He hadn't been able to understand her at first, but had quickly surmised through her distress that her stalker was there and he was hurting Rosa and Fiona.

She had hung up before he could ask any questions and he had assumed she was calling 911 as he heard the call go out of an assault while he was en route, screaming through town with lights and sirens blazing.

The door opened. "I'm here," Jenna said. "I sent Addie into our apartment. Oh, Rosa. You saved us."

She wrapped her arms around her friend and Wyatt didn't miss the way Rosa winced. She had more aches and pains than just the bloody lip he could see.

The bastard was bleeding, too, from what looked like a nasty contusion. Wyatt looked around and found a large rock with blood on it. Had Rosa hit him with that? Good for her.

He finished handcuffing Barker and read him his rights, all while the man kept babbling about being a police officer and how this was all a big mistake.

"Tell them, Jenna. Tell them you love me."

The woman looked down at the man who had so tormented her, driving her away from her home with his obsession.

"I despise you," she said clearly. "I hope you rot in hell."

Barker made a move toward her but Wyatt yanked the restraint.

"We can straighten everything out down at the station," Wyatt said, just as backup officers arrived to help him secure the scene.

Only after they had taken custody of the man and another officer started taking Jenna's statement about the incident and the months of torment preceding it could Wyatt finally go to Rosa, who was now sitting on the porch steps.

She forced a smile when he approached and he saw her lip was cracked and swollen.

"He hurt you." He reached a hand out and tenderly caressed her face.

She let out a little sob and sagged into his arms. He held her, burying his face in her hair as he tried not to think about what might have happened to her.

How would he have endured it? He had already lost one woman he loved. He couldn't stand the idea of losing another.

"I am all right," she murmured. "Jenna is safe. That is the important thing. But I have to take Fiona to the vet. That man kicked her. She was so brave."

They both were incredibly brave. He looked over her shoulder, where Fiona's tail was wagging.

She almost looked like she was smiling as the two of them embraced. "She seems okay to me."

Rosa drew away a little and he instantly wanted to pull her back into his arms.

"I would still like to have her checked out. The veterinarian is my friend. I will call her."

An ambulance pulled up, followed by a fire truck. The whole town was coming to her rescue, which was only proof about how well-regarded Rosa was in town.

Right behind them, a couple he recognized came racing up the driveway.

"Rosa!" Melissa Sanderson exclaimed. "What happened? We saw all the police racing past and hurried right over."

"I am fine," Rosa said. "A man came to hurt Jen but she and Addie were able to get to safety."

"Because of you," Jenna said as she approached with her daughter in her arms. "You saved us."

She hugged her friend again and Wyatt could see Rosa was trying not to wince.

"You look like you've gone a few rounds with a heavyweight champion." Melissa's husband, Eli, a physician in town, looked concerned. "You should let me have a look."

Rosa, his battered warrior, glowered at them all. "This is all too much fuss for a sore lip."

"He kicked her in the back, too," Jenna said.

"At least once. Maybe more. I don't know. I was so scared."

"You need to go to the ER," Wyatt said.

She shook her head. "Not until Fiona sees the veterinarian."

"You can at least let Eli and the paramedics check you out while I call the veterinarian," Wyatt said.

She gave him a grateful look. "Yes. I will do that. Thank you."

Chapter Sixteen

To his deep regret, that was the last chance he had to talk to her for the next few hours. He didn't want to leave, but as the on-scene arresting officer, he had paperwork and an investigation to deal with.

He had tried to interrogate Barker but the man was sleeping off what appeared to be a large quantity of alcohol, as well as a concussion delivered by Rosa and her trusty rock and several dog bites from Fiona.

By the time he left the station, the sun was beginning to set.

He knew from the other officers on scene that Rosa had refused transport to the hospital, though she had allowed Eli to clean and bandage her cuts.

Stubborn woman.

Only now, as he walked up the front steps to the house hours later, did Wyatt feel his own adrenaline crash.

He had never been so scared as the moment when Jenna had called him, her voice thready with panic. All he had registered were her words that Rosa was being hurt.

It seemed odd to be here without either Hank or Logan, but Carrie had offered to keep both of them overnight.

"You do what you need to for Jen and Rosa," she had told him when he called from the station. She had been half out of her mind with worry for her friend and only his repeated assurances that Rosa's injuries appeared to be minor had kept Carrie from rushing to the house herself.

He half expected to find Rosa in the flower gardens around Brambleberry House, seeking peace and solace amid the blossoms and the birds, as she so often did. But from what he could see, the gardens were empty except for a few hummingbirds at the bright red feeder. They immediately flitted away.

The big house also seemed quiet when he let himself inside. He walked to the third floor and knocked, but Rosa didn't answer. He couldn't hear Fiona inside, either.

He frowned, not sure what to do.

As he headed back down the stairs, the door on the second-floor landing opened. Jenna peeked out. "I thought I heard you come in."

"Yeah. How are you?"

"I've had better days."

"It has to help to know that Barker is in custody, doesn't it?"

She shrugged and he could see she wasn't entirely convinced her nightmare was over. He couldn't blame her for the doubt after the way the system had already treated her, but Wyatt was quick to reassure her.

"You should know that Barker won't be going anywhere for a long time. He's facing extensive state and federal charges. And we haven't even started on the stalking charges. That will only add to his sentence. He won't bother you again."

"I hope not."

He knew it would probably take time for that reality to sink in.

"Is Rosa with you?"

"No. I heard her take Fiona out about a half hour ago."

She paused. "I never wanted her to get hurt. I hope you know that. I thought we would be safe here. If I had for a moment dreamed he would find me and would come here and hurt Rosa and Fiona, I never would have come."

"I know that and I'm sure Rosa doesn't blame you for a second."

Jenna didn't look convinced about this, either. "She was amazing. I wish you could have seen her. She was so fierce. Aaron was twice as big, but that didn't stop her. She's an incredible woman."

"Agreed," he said, his voice gruff.

"She risked her life to protect me and Addie." Jenna's voice took on an edge and she gave him a hard stare. "For the record, I will do the same for her. Anybody who hurts her in any possible way will live to regret it."

Was that a threat? It certainly sounded like one. He couldn't decide whether to be offended that she could ever think he would hurt Rosa, or touched at her loyalty to her friend. He settled on the latter.

"You and I are the same in that sentiment, then," he said quietly.

She studied his features for a moment, then nodded. "I saw her from my window as I was putting Addie to bed. She and Fiona appeared to be heading for the beach."

He smiled and on impulse reached out and hugged her. After a surprised moment, Jenna hugged him back.

He headed for the beach gate, his heart pounding. As he went, he carried on a fierce debate with himself.

Rosa had basically ordered him to keep his dis-

tance and told him she wasn't interested in a relationship. He had tried his best. For a week, he
had worked long hours at his house so that he and
Logan could move out as soon as possible. The
whole time, he had done his best to push her out
of his head and his heart.

It hadn't worked.

The moment Jenna had called him in a panic,
the moment he knew they were in danger, Wyatt
had realized nothing had changed. He was in love
with Rosa and would move heaven and earth to
keep her safe.

He pushed open the beach gate and found her
there, just beyond the house. She was sitting on a
blanket on the sand, her arm around Fiona and her
back to him as she watched the sun slipping down
into the water in a blaze of color.

She didn't hear him come out at first. Fiona did.
The dog turned to look at him, but apparently decided he was no threat because she nestled closer
to her human.

He moved across the sand, still not sure what
he would say to her, only knowing he had to be
close to her, too.

He saw the moment she registered his presence.
Her spine stiffened and she turned her head. He
couldn't see her expression behind her sunglasses.

"Oh. Hello."

"Here you are. I was worried about you."

"Yes. We are here. The sunset seems especially beautiful tonight."

He had to agree. Streaks of pink and purple and orange spilled out in glorious Technicolor. "May I join you?"

She hesitated. He could see her jaw flex, as if she wanted to say no, but she finally gestured to the empty spot on the blanket, which happened to be on the other side of her dog.

He would have liked to be next to Rosa, but this would do, he supposed.

"Where are Logan and Hank?"

"They were both with Carrie when Jenna called me. After Carrie heard what happened to you and found out I was part of the investigation, she insisted they stay the night with her."

"Ah."

He reached out and rubbed her brave, amazing dog behind the ear. His hand brushed against Rosa's and it hurt a little when she pulled her hand away.

"How's Fiona?"

"Fine. Dr. Williams said she might be a little bruised, but nothing appears to be broken. I am to watch her appetite and her energy over the next few days and tell her if I see anything unusual."

"You're a good, brave girl, aren't you?" He scratched Fi under the chin and the dog rested her head on his leg.

All the emotions he had put away in the heat of the moment as he did his duty and stood for justice seemed to come rushing over him again, all at once.

"What you did—protecting your friend. It was incredibly brave."

She gave a short laugh. "I think you mean to say stupid."

"I would never say that. Never. You were amazing."

He reached for her hand, unable to help himself. He thought she would pull away again, but she didn't. Her fingers were cool and seemed to be trembling a little, but he couldn't say whether that was from the cool coastal air or from the trauma of earlier.

She drew in a breath that sounded ragged, and before he quite realized it, she let out a sob and then another.

Oh, Rosa.

His poor, fierce Rosa.

Fiona, blessed Fiona, moved out of the way so that Wyatt could pull Rosa into his arms. He held her while she cried silently against his chest, not making a sound except the occasional whimper.

His heart ached for her, both for the fear she must have felt and for everything else she had endured.

"I am sorry," she finally said, sounding mortified. "I think I have been holding that in all afternoon."

"Or longer."

She shifted her face to meet his gaze. Somehow, she had lost her sunglasses and he could see her now, her eyes dark and shadowed in her lovely face. Instead of answering his unspoken question, she focused on the events of the day.

"I was so frightened. I thought this man, he was going to kill me, then get to Jenna and Addie. I could not let him."

"He won't get to Jenna now. He is in custody and will be charged with assault, trespassing, drunk driving, driving across state lines with the intent to commit a felony and a whole host of other charges related to whatever stalking charges we can prove. He's not going to get out for a long time."

"I hope that is the case."

"It is," he promised. He would do whatever necessary to make sure of it.

"I suppose I should be relieved I did not kill him with that rock."

"You were pretty fierce."

"I could not help it. I could only think about protecting Jenna and Addie from someone who wanted to hurt them. Something seemed to take over me. Maybe some part of my brain that was fifteen years old again, focused only on surviving another day."

As soon as she said the words, she looked as if she wished she hadn't. She closed her eyes. He thought she would pull away from him but she didn't. She continued to nestle against him as if he was providing safe shelter in a sandstorm.

With his thumb, he brushed away a tear that trickled down her cheek, his heart a heavy ache. "Tell me what happened when you were fifteen."

"I have already told you too much. I don't talk about that time in my life, Wyatt. It is the past and has nothing to do with who I am now."

"You don't have to tell me. I understand if you prefer to keep it to yourself. But I hope you know you can trust me, if you ever change your mind."

She eased away from him and sat once more on the blanket beside him. Fiona moved to her other side and plopped next to her. Rosa wrapped her arms around her knees and gazed out at the water, a pale blue in the twilight.

She was silent for a long time, so long that he thought she wasn't going to answer. But then she looked at him out of the corner of her gaze and he fell in love with her all over again.

"Sometimes it feels like it all happened to someone else. Something I read about in a terribly tragic novel."

He did not want to hear what was coming next,

but somehow Wyatt sensed it was important to both of them that she tell him. This was the reason she had pushed him away. He was suddenly certain of it.

That moment when he had rushed onto the porch earlier, he had seen raw emotion in her expression. That was the image he couldn't get out of his head. She had looked at him with relief, with gratitude and with something else, too.

She thought her past was a barrier between them. If he could show her it wasn't, that together they could face whatever demons she fought, perhaps she would stop pushing him away.

"I told you about the men who offered me a job in this country and who…brought me here."

"Yes."

"It was not a factory job they were bringing me to, as I thought. I was so stupid."

"I didn't think it was."

She closed her eyes. "You are a detective. I am sure you can guess what happened next."

"I've imagined a few possible scenarios since the night you told me."

"Pick the worst one and you might be close enough."

He gripped her hand tightly, not wanting to ever let go. "Human trafficking."

She made a small sound. "Yes. That is a polite phrase for it. I was brought here to work in the sex trade. Me, an innocent girl from a small town who had never even kissed a boy. I barely knew what sex was."

Everything inside him went cold as he thought about what she must have endured. "Oh, sweetheart. I'm so sorry."

"I refused at first. The men who brought me here, they did not care whether I was willing or not."

How was it possible for his heart to break again and again?

"You were raped."

She looked at him, stark pain in her eyes. "Now you know why I don't like thinking about the past. Yes. I was raped. At first by the men who wanted to use me to make money for them. Then by some of their customers. I did not cooperate. Not one single time. They threatened me, hurt me, tried to make me take drugs like the other girls, so I would be quiet and do what they said. I would not. I only cried. All the time."

"That couldn't have been good for business."

She gave a short, humorless laugh. "No. Not at all. Finally, they left me alone. I still do not know why they did not kill me. It would have been easy for them. But then one of the girls died of too much drugs. She was…not well, so they had let her do all the cooking and cleaning for the other girls. They let me take her place. At least I no longer had to let strangers touch me."

He squeezed her fingers. How had she possibly emerged from that hell still able to smile and laugh and find joy in the world, with a gentle spirit and a kind heart? Most people would have curled up and withered away in the midst of so much trauma.

"This went on for a few months and then I made a mistake. I knew I had to do something to change my situation. I could not stay. I tried to escape but they...caught me. They would have killed me that night. They knew I could tell the police who they were. I expected to die. I thought I would. But somehow, I did not. I do not know why. I only knew I had to do all I could to survive. Mine was not the only life at risk that night."

"One of your friends?"

She gave a tiny shake of her head and gazed out at the undulating waves. He waited for her to explain. When she did not, suddenly all his suspicions came together and he knew. He didn't know how. He just did.

"You were pregnant."

She met his gaze, her expression filled with sadness and pain. "No one else knew. I did not even know myself until I was too far along to—to do anything. I told you I was innocent."

"How did you get away?"

She shrugged. "A miracle from God. That is the only thing it could have been."

He had never heard her being particularly religious but the conviction in her voice seemed unswerving. He would take her word for it, since he hadn't been there.

"We were kept above a restaurant in a tourist town in Utah. They left me to die in a room there, but I did not. I had only pretended. After they left, I saw they had not locked the door, like usual. They thought I was dead. Why should they?"

How badly had she been hurt? Wyatt didn't even want to contemplate. And she'd only been a child. Not much older than his niece. How had she endured it?

"Somehow, I found strength to stand and managed to go out, stumbling down the back stairs. I still cannot believe they did not hear me. Once I was out, I did not know what to do. Where to go. I knew no one. I was certain I only had moments before they found me and finished what they had started, so I... I somehow climbed into the back of a truck."

"With a stranger?"

He thought of all the things that could have happened to her by putting her trust in someone she did not know. On the other hand, she was escaping certain death so she probably thought anything was better than the place she was leaving.

"I was lucky. There was a blanket there for the horses and I was able to pull it over me so I did not freeze. The man was a rancher. He did not spot me until we were away from town, when he had a flat tire and found me sleeping."

"What did he do?" Wyatt was again almost afraid to ask.

"He called the police and a kind sheriff and a doctor came to my rescue. Daniel and Lauren. My parents."

Chapter Seventeen

Rosa could feel herself trembling, though the night was pleasant. She knew it was probably a delayed reaction from the attack earlier and from the emotional trauma of reliving the darkest time in her life.

When Wyatt wrapped his arm around her and pulled her close to his heat, she wanted to sink into him. He was big, safe and comforting, and offered immeasurable strength.

She could not tell by his expression what he thought about what she had told him. She thought maybe that wasn't such a bad thing. Did she want to know what he was thinking about her?

"They took you in."

"They were not married at the time. Not even together. I like to think I helped them find each other. But, yes. Lauren took me home with her. I was still in danger. I had information about the men who took me. I knew who they were, where they were, so I—I stayed with Lauren until all the men were caught."

"All of them?" Wyatt's voice had a hard note she had not heard before, as if he wanted to go to Utah right now and find justice for her.

Oh, he was a dear man. A little more warmth seeped into her heart. How was she supposed to resist him?

"Yes. Some were deported. Others are still in jail here in this country. Daniel made sure all the girls were rescued and the men were punished."

"I would like to meet Sheriff Galvez," he said gruffly.

"You two are similar. I think you would be friends. That is one reason why I..." Her voice trailed off and she felt her face heat, as she was unable to complete the sentence. *Why I fell in love with you.*

"Why you what?"

"Nothing," she said quickly. "I only wanted to tell you, after Daniel and Lauren married, they gave me a home and then legally adopted me."

"They sound wonderful."

"The best. Though they can be too protective of me."

"That's understandable, don't you think?"

She nodded. "Yes. I do understand but this is one reason I think I had to move somewhere else. Somewhere I would not be poor Rosa Galvez."

"What about your baby?" he asked.

Ah. Here was the most difficult part. The other things that had happened—the abuse, the beatings. Even the rapes. Those scars had healed. She hardly thought of them anymore.

Her child. That was a wound that would never close completely.

She chose her words carefully, wishing she did not have to tell him this part. "I had a baby girl ten weeks later and…she was adopted."

There. The words still burned her throat.

He was quiet for a long time. Was he recoiling now from her? She could not blame him. It had been a terrible choice for someone who had been little more than a child to have to make.

"It's Bella, isn't it? Your daughter?"

That was the last thing she expected him to say. In horror, she jerked away and scrambled to her feet. Fiona immediately moved to her side, as if sensing more danger.

"No! Bella? How ridiculous! Do not say this. You are crazy."

He rose, as well, gazing at her across the sand.

The rising moon lit up one side of his face, leaving the other in shadow. "I'm not crazy though, am I?" he said quietly. "I'm right."

She didn't know what to say. How could she convince him he had made a terrible mistake? She had no words to undo this.

"No. This is not true," she said, but even she could hear her words lacked conviction. "I do not know how... Why did you think of this?"

"The time frame lines up. Bella is the right age and she was adopted through your aunt Anna. You're her birth mother." If her own words lacked conviction, his did not. He spoke with a growing confidence she had no way to combat.

"I don't know why I didn't see the resemblance before. Maybe I didn't want to see it. Does she know?"

Rosa stared at him, not sure what to say. All of her instincts were shouting at her to go inside the safety of the house, but she couldn't leave. She had started this by telling him her history. It was her fault. He was a police detective. How could she blame him for connecting all the pieces of the jigsaw and coming up with the correct picture?

This was the part of the story she did not want him to know. The part she had been trying to protect him from. What must he think of her now? She had abandoned his niece, a girl he loved. She had given birth and handed her over to another woman to be her mother, then went on with her life. Learning English. Finishing school. Dating boys. Going to college.

Why did he not seem angry? Why was he looking at her like that, with a tender light in his eyes? Did he not understand what she had done?

She could not think about that now. For this moment, she had to focus on controlling the damage she had done. She should not have told him anything. Since she had, now she had to make sure he did not ruin all the care she had taken during the years she had lived in Cannon Beach, so close to her daughter but still far enough away.

"No. She does not know," she finally said. "And you cannot tell her. Oh, please. Do not tell her."

"I would never, if you don't want me to."

"You must promise me. Swear it."

He seemed to blink at her vehemence, but then nodded. "I swear. I won't tell her. This is not my secret to tell, Rosa. Again, please trust me enough to know I would never betray you."

Oh, she wanted to trust him. The urge to step back into his arms was so overpowering, she had to wrap her own arms around herself to keep from doing it. "I thank you. She might have come from an ugly time in my life but none of that was her fault. She is the most beautiful, precious girl. From the moment I felt her move inside me, I loved her.

I wanted so much to keep her but it was… It was impossible."

"You were only a child yourself."

"Yes. What would I do with a baby? I had no way to take care of her myself, though I wanted to."

"It's obvious you love her. Whether she knows the truth or not, there is a bond between you."

"How could anyone not love her? Bella is wonderful. Smart and pretty, always kind. She reminds me of my mother."

"That's funny. She reminds me of *her* mother, now that I know who she is."

She blushed at the intensity in her voice. "Carrie is her mother. She has loved her and cared for her far better than I ever could."

"Do Joe and Carrie know?"

"Yes. Of course. I would not have come here without telling them. When Anna asked me to come to help her with the store, I knew I must tell Carrie and Joe first. I called them to see how they might feel if I moved to town. I did not want to cause them any tension or discomfort."

"What did they say?"

"They welcomed me. They have always been so kind to me. Always. From the day we met in the hospital. They never once made me feel as if I had…done something wrong."

"Because you hadn't!"

She sighed. It was easy for others to say that. They had not lived her journey. "I know that most of the time but sometimes I do wonder. I made foolish choices. Dangerous choices. And because of that, an innocent child was born."

He reached for her hands again and curled his fingers around hers. To Rosa's shock, he lifted her hands and pressed first one hand to his mouth and then the other.

"You did nothing wrong, Rosa. *Nothing.* You were an innocent child yourself, looking for a brighter future. You couldn't have known what would happen to you."

Tears spilled out again at his words and the healing balm they offered. He was not disgusted by her story. She did not know why. It seemed the second miracle of her life.

He pulled her back into his arms. She knew she should try to be strong but she couldn't. Not right now. She would try to find the strength later to restore distance between them but right now she needed the heat and comfort of him. She wrapped her arms around his waist and rested her head against his chest again, wishing she could stay here forever.

"If Carrie and Joe know the truth, why doesn't Bella?"

Thinking about it made her stomach hurt. This

was her greatest fear. Every day, she worried Bella would learn the truth and would come to hate her.

"They wanted to tell her but I—I begged them not to. I thought it would be better for her if I could be in her life only as a friend. Maybe like a sort of…older sister or cousin."

"Why would that be better?"

She shrugged against him. "How do I tell her that she was created through an act of violence at a time in my life I wish I could forget?"

"You wouldn't have to tell her that part."

"What do I say when she asks me about her father? I did not know how I could answer that. I still do not know. How can I tell her I do not even know his name? No. It is better that she not know the truth."

His silence told her he didn't agree.

"When I came here, I did not want to intrude in her life," she said. "Carrie and Joe are her parents in every way that matters and they have been wonderful to her. I only wanted to…see her. Make sure she was happy. Healthy. I thought I would only be here a short time but then I came to love her and to love Cannon Beach and Brambleberry House. Anna offered me a partnership in the store and it became harder to think about leaving."

"I am glad you stayed. So glad," he said. And before she realized what he intended, he lowered his mouth and kissed her with a sweetness and gentleness that took her breath.

Her mouth still burned where she had been hit, but she ignored it, lost in the peace and wonder of kissing the man she loved on a moonswept beach.

He still wanted to kiss her, after everything she told him. All this time, she had been so afraid for him to learn the truth. He now knew the ugliest part of her past and yet he kissed her anyway with a tenderness that made her feel…cherished.

"Thank you for coming to my rescue." She realized in that moment she had not really told him that yet. And while she was speaking about earlier, with Aaron Barker, her words held layers of meaning.

He smiled against her mouth. "I don't think you needed help from me. You were doing just fine. You're pretty ferocious, Rosita."

The endearment—Little Rosa—made her smile, too. Her mother had always called her that and Daniel still did.

"Ow. Smiling still hurts."

"Oh. I forgot about your mouth. I shouldn't have kissed you. I'm sorry."

"I am glad you did." To prove it, she pressed her mouth, sore lip and all, to his.

All of the emotions she could not say were contained in that kiss. All the love and yearning she had been fighting for so long.

When he lifted his head, Wyatt was breathing hard and Rosa realized they were once more on the sand, sitting on the blanket she had brought.

"I have to tell you something," Wyatt said after a long moment. He gripped her hands again, and even through the darkness, she could see the intense light in his eyes.

"I was scared to death when Jenna called me and said you were in trouble. I made all kinds of deals with God on my way to Brambleberry House, begging Him to keep you safe until I could get here."

"You...did?" She didn't know what to say, shaken to her core by the emotion in his voice. Her heart, already beating hard from the kiss, seemed to race even faster.

"Yes. Though I suppose I should have known you could take care of yourself," he said with a little smile. "You're amazing, Rosa. One of the most amazing women I have ever met."

She could not seem to wrap her mind around this man speaking such tender, wonderful words.

"I do not understand," she finally asked. "How can you say that after—after everything I have told you about my past? About what I had to do? About...about giving my baby to someone else?"

"All of those things only make me love you more."

She thought she must have misheard him.

"Love me. You cannot love me." She stared through the darkness, wishing she could see him better. She wanted to drag him back to the house so she could look at him in the light to read the truth.

"Yet I do," he said, his voice ringing with so much truth she had to believe him. "What you did was remarkable. Even more so because of what you have been through. You were scared to death but you still risked your life to protect your friend. You make me ashamed of myself."

"Ashamed? Why? You came as soon as you heard we were in danger."

"I don't have your kind of courage. I have been fighting falling in love with you for a long time. I think long before I moved to Brambleberry House."

"Why?" She was still not sure she could believe it but she wanted to. Oh, she wanted to.

"I loved my wife," he said simply. "When she died, I thought I had nothing else to give. I did not want to love someone else. Love brought too much pain and sadness and it was easier, safer, to keep my heart locked away."

He kissed her gently, on the side of her mouth that had not been hurt. "I am not brave like a certain woman I know who has endured horrible things but still manages to be kind and cheerful and loving."

His words soaked through her, more comforting than she could ever tell him.

"This woman. She sounds very annoying. Too good to be true."

He laughed. "She isn't. She's amazing. Did I tell you that she also reaches out to those in need and is willing to protect them with every fierce ounce of her being?"

She was not the perfect woman he was describing. But hearing how he saw her made her want to be.

Wasn't that what love should be? A window that allowed you to discover the best in yourself because someone else saw you that way?

She didn't know. She only knew she loved Wyatt with all her heart and wanted a future with him, as she had never wanted anything in her life.

"I know something about this woman that you might not," she said.

"What's that?"

The words seemed to catch in her throat as those demons of self-doubt whispered in her ear. No. She would not listen to them. This was too important.

"This woman. She very much loves a certain police detective. She has loved him for a long time, too. Probably since he moved to town with his sad eyes and his beautiful little boy."

He gazed down at her, those eyes no longer sad

but blazing with light, joy and wonder. "Well. That works out then, doesn't it?"

He kissed her again, his arms wrapped tightly around her. Her entire journey had been leading her to this moment, she realized. This moment and this man who knew all her secrets and loved her despite them. Or maybe a little because of them.

She loved Wyatt. She wanted a future with him and with Logan. Thinking about that boy who already held such a big part of her heart only added to her happiness.

She could clearly picture that future together, filled with laughter and joy. Kisses and Spanish lessons and walks along the beach with their dogs.

She had no doubt that it would be rich and beautiful, full and joyous and rewarding. The scent of freesia drifted across the sand and Rosa smiled, happy to know that Abigail approved.

Epilogue

One year later

What a glorious day for a wedding.

Rosa woke just as the sun was beginning to creep over the horizon in her third-floor apartment of Brambleberry House.

She stayed in bed for a moment, anticipation shivering through her. For a few disoriented moments, she wasn't sure why, then she caught sight of Fiona's head on the bed, the dog watching her intently, and she remembered.

Today was the day. This day, she was marrying Wyatt and becoming Logan's stepmother.

In a few short hours, they would stand in the

gardens of Brambleberry House and exchange their vows.

Everyone was in town. Her parents, Anna and Harry, Sonia Elizabeth and her husband, Luke.

Fiona made the little sound she did when she wanted to go for a walk and Rosa had to smile.

"I am not even out of bed yet. You really want a walk now?"

The dog continued to give her a steady look she could not ignore.

With a sigh, she slipped out of bed, threw on sweats and a baseball cap and then put on Fiona's leash. A moment later, they headed down the stairs of Brambleberry House.

This was her last morning in this apartment and her last morning as Rosa Vallejo Galvez. Tonight she would be Rosa Vallejo Galvez Townsend.

A wife and a mother.

After their honeymoon, she and Wyatt would be returning to the ground-floor apartment of Brambleberry House. They had decided to stay here for now.

He was going to rent out his small bungalow and they would move to the larger apartment, with its sunroom and extra bedroom. It was larger than his house, plus had extensive grounds where Logan could play, as well as his best friend, Addie, living upstairs.

She knew it wouldn't last. At some point, they

would probably want to find a house of their own. For now, she was glad she did not have to leave the house completely.

She knew it was silly but Rosa felt like Bramble-berry House was excited about the upcoming wedding and all the coming changes. She seemed to smell flowers all the time and wondered if Abigail was flitting through the house, watching all the preparations.

The summer morning was beautiful, with wisps of sea mist curling up through the trees. It was cool now but she knew the afternoon would be perfect for a garden wedding overlooking the sea.

The decorations were already in place and she admired them as she walked through with Fi toward the beach gate.

Fiona, usually well-behaved, was tugging on the leash as Rosa walked onto the sand. She lunged toward a few other early-morning beach walkers, which was completely not like her.

It looked like a man and a child walking a little dog, but they were too far away for her to see them clearly. Suddenly Fiona broke free of Rosa's hold and raced toward them, dragging her leash behind her.

The boy, who Rosa was now close enough to recognize as a nearly eight-year-old boy with a blond cowlick and his father's blue eyes, caught Fiona's leash and came hurrying toward Rosa.

"Rosa! *Buenos*, Rosa!"

"Buenos, mijo." When he reached her, he hugged her hard and Rosa's simmering joy seemed to bubble over.

A few more hours and they would be a family.

A year ago, she never could have imagined this day for herself. She expected she would be content going to other people's weddings. She would dance, laugh, enjoy the refreshments and then go home trying to ignore the pang of loneliness.

Destined to be alone. That is what she had always thought.

She could not have been happier to be so very wrong.

"I don't think I'm supposed to see you today. Isn't it bad luck?" Wyatt's voice was gruff but his eyes blazed with so much tenderness and love, she felt tears of happiness gather in hers. He always made her feel so cherished.

"I think you are not supposed to see me in the wedding dress. I do not think the superstition means you cannot see me in my old sweatpants, when I have barely combed my hair and look terrible. Anyway, I do not care about such things. We make our own luck, right?"

He laughed and reached for her. "Yes. I guess we do. To be safe, I won't tell Carrie and Bella we bumped in to you on our walk. They *do* care about that kind of thing."

Rosa smiled and her heart seemed to sigh when he kissed her, his mouth warm and firm against the morning chill.

"You do not have to tell me. I have heard every superstition about weddings from them since the day we became engaged."

"I don't know how it's possible, but I think Bella is even more excited about this wedding than we are."

Rosa smiled, adding even more happiness to her overflowing cup when she thought of his niece. Her niece, after today.

And her daughter.

After talking with Joe and Carrie several months earlier, she had decided she must tell Bella the truth.

They had all sat down together and, gathering her courage and without giving all the grim details, Rosa had told Bella she was her birth mother.

To her shock, Bella had simply shrugged. "And?" she had said. "I've only known that, like, forever."

"You have not!" Rosa had said, shocked nearly speechless. "How?"

"It wasn't exactly hard to figure out. You just have to look at a selfie of us together. We look enough alike to be sisters."

"Why didn't you say anything?" Carrie had looked and sounded as shocked as Rosa.

"I figured you all would say something eventually when you wanted me to know. What's the big deal? You're like one of my best friends, anyway."

Rosa had burst into tears at that and so had Carrie.

Nothing seemed to have changed between them. Bella still confided in her about boys she liked, and Rosa still tried to be like a wise older sister.

In that time, Bella had never asked about her father. Maybe some day, when she was older, Rosa would figure out a way to tell her something. For now, she was grateful every day for the bright, beautiful daughter who seemed happy to let her into her life.

"She has done a great job of helping me plan the wedding. I would have been lost without her," she said now to Wyatt.

Bella was one of her bridesmaids and could not have been more excited to help her work out every detail of the wedding, from the cake to the dresses to the food at the reception. In fact, Rosa thought she might have a good future as a wedding planner, if she wanted.

"I'm sure she's done a great job," he said. "It's going to be a beautiful day. But not nearly as gorgeous as you."

She smiled as he kissed her again. A loud sigh finally distracted them both. "Can we be done kissing now? You guys are gross."

"Sorry, kid." Wyatt smiled down at his son but made no move to release her. "We both kind of like it."

That was an understatement. They were magic together. She loved his kiss, his touch, and could not wait until she could wake up each morning in his arms.

"Fiona and Hank want to take a walk," Logan informed them. "So do I."

Wyatt kissed Rosa firmly one more time then drew away. "Fine," he said. "But you'd better get used to the kissing, kid."

He reached for Rosa's hand and the three of them and their dogs walked down the beach while gulls cried and the waves washed against the shore.

The perfect day and the perfect life seemed to stretch out ahead of them and Rosa knew she had everything she could ever need, right here.

* * * * *

WE HOPE YOU ENJOYED
THIS BOOK FROM

◆ HARLEQUIN
SPECIAL
EDITION

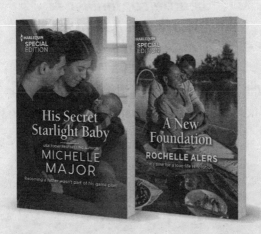

Believe in love. Overcome obstacles. Find happiness.

Relate to finding comfort and strength in the
support of loved ones and enjoy the journey
no matter what life throws your way.

6 NEW BOOKS AVAILABLE EVERY MONTH!

HARLEQUIN

*Uplifting or passionate,
heartfelt or thrilling—
Harlequin has your
happily-ever-after.*

With a wide range of romance series that each
offer new books every month, you are sure to
find the satisfying escape you deserve.

**Look for all Harlequin series
new releases on the
last Tuesday of each month
in stores and online!**

Harlequin.com

"Even the strongest people need a break now and then. It's
not a sign of being weak—it's part of being human," he
murmured against her temple. "As far as I'm concerned,
you're a badass."

She shook her head but didn't say anything.

"Look at your girls," he insisted. "You put those smiles
on their faces. You found a way to keep them entertained
and positive and with enough imagination to turn that
leaning wooden shack into a playhouse—"

"Hey," she interrupted, peering up at him with red-
rimmed eyes.

"I was teasing." He smiled. "You're missing the point
here."

"Oh?" She didn't seem fazed by the fact that she was still holding on to him—or that there was barely any space between them.

But he was. And it had him reeling. The moment her gaze met his, the tightness and pressure in his chest gave way. And having Skylar in his arms, soft and warm and all woman, was something he hadn't prepared himself for.

Focus. Not on the unnerving reaction Skylar was causing, but on being here for Skylar and the girls. *Focus on honoring Chad's last request.* Chad—who'd expected him to take care of the family he'd left behind, not get blindsided and want more than he should. How could he not? Skylar was a strong, beautiful woman who had his heart thumping in a way he didn't recognize.

"Thank you, again." Her gaze swept over his face before she rose on tiptoe and kissed his cheek. "You're a good man, Kyle Mitchell."

Don't miss
Their Rancher Protector *by Sasha Summers,*
available August 2021 wherever
Harlequin Special Edition *books and ebooks are sold.*

Harlequin.com

Love Harlequin romance?

DISCOVER.

Be the first to find out about promotions, news and exclusive content!

Facebook.com/HarlequinBooks

Twitter.com/HarlequinBooks

Instagram.com/HarlequinBooks

Pinterest.com/HarlequinBooks

ReaderService.com

EXPLORE.

Sign up for the Harlequin e-newsletter and download a free book from any series at **TryHarlequin.com**

CONNECT.

Join our Harlequin community to share your thoughts and connect with other romance readers!
Facebook.com/groups/HarlequinConnection